New York Bachelors' Club

Time to change their minds?

Through thick and thin, Dr. Kaleb Sabat and
Dr. Snowden Tangredi have *always* had each other's
backs. So, when life—or, rather, love!—hits them
hard, they make a vow. No more relationships!

But just as soon as they promise to be lifelong
bachelors, two *incredible* women arrive at their
hospital…ready to rewrite the New York
bachelors' rules!

Meet the staff of
New York Memorial Hospital with…

Kaleb and Nicola's Story
Consequences of Their New York Night

Snowden and Kirsten's Story
The Trouble with the Tempting Doc

Available now!

Dear Reader,

There are times in our lives when we just want to pick up and start over. Or is that just me?

Well, it's definitely the case with transplant surgeon Snowden Tangredi. Newly single, he is ready for a fresh start. A start that doesn't involve relationships of any kind. The day he signs his divorce papers, he and his childhood friend decide they are no longer looking for any kind of Ms. Right. And Snow has another reason for keeping his distance from people. He carries a secret, one he kept from even his ex-wife.

Except Kirsten Nadif comes along and makes him want to lance a wound that has festered for years. Thank you for joining Snow and Kirsten as they discover that trust isn't as far out of reach as they think it is. It might even be standing right beside them. I will admit this story made me cry as I wrote it. I hope you love it as much as I do. Happy reading!

Love,

Tina Beckett

THE TROUBLE WITH
THE TEMPTING DOC

TINA BECKETT

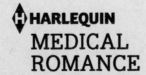

HARLEQUIN
MEDICAL
ROMANCE

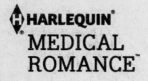

HARLEQUIN®
MEDICAL ROMANCE™

Recycling programs for this product may not exist in your area.

ISBN-13: 978-1-335-40441-1

The Trouble with the Tempting Doc

Harlequin Enterprises ULC
22 Adelaide St. West, 40th Floor
Toronto, Ontario M5H 4E3, Canada
www.Harlequin.com

Printed in U.S.A.

Three-times Golden Heart® Award finalist **Tina Beckett** learned to pack her suitcases almost before she learned to read. Born to a military family, she has lived in the United States, Puerto Rico, Portugal and Brazil. In addition to traveling, Tina loves to cuddle with her pug, Alex, spend time with her family and hit the trails on her horse. Learn more about Tina from her website, or friend her on Facebook.

Books by Tina Beckett

Harlequin Medical Romance

A Summer in São Paulo
One Hot Night with Dr. Cardoza
London Hospital Midwives
Miracle Baby for the Midwife
Hope Children's Hospital
The Billionaire's Christmas Wish
Hot Greek Docs
Tempted by Dr. Patera

The Doctors' Baby Miracle
One Night to Change Their Lives
The Surgeon's Surprise Baby
A Family to Heal His Heart
A Christmas Kiss with Her Ex-Army Doc
Risking It All for the Children's Doc
It Started with a Winter Kiss

Visit the Author Profile page
at Harlequin.com for more titles.

PROLOGUE

SNOWDEN TANGREDI STOOD at the front of the church and adjusted his bow tie. It didn't work. It still felt tight—constrictive—and made him aware of the pulse that pounded in his neck. In his head. In his chest.

The front of a church was definitely not a place he ever saw himself standing again. But at least this time the officiant wasn't there for him. No, the victim this time was his best friend, Kaleb Sabat.

Then again, Kaleb said he'd never walk this path, either. In fact, they'd made a boozy pact to that effect almost a year ago. And yet here Kaleb was, waiting on his bride-to-be.

Some people might have said Kaleb had no choice—that having a baby had put the stamp of fatherhood on his head—but Snow knew his buddy well enough to know that he didn't do anything unless he wanted to. He was one of the most stubborn men Snow knew. But he was also one of the most upright and honest. And loyal to a fault.

His friend glanced his way and gave a half grin that said everything. Their pact to remain bachelors for life was about to be ripped to shreds. And while there was a rueful element to Kaleb's look, there was not an ounce of regret accompanying it. The man was head over heels for Nicola and his new baby girl. And Nicola seemed to love him just as fiercely.

But for how long? How long before reality set in and the newness wore off?

Snow's one jaunt down an aisle very much like this one had been full of the same air of expectation and hope. And healing. Or so he thought. If only he'd known then what he knew now. That the healing he'd hoped for had never materialized. Instead, a gnawing fear had crouched in the background, waiting for him to become the slightest bit irritated or angry. Then it came out to play, claws unsheathed. He soon realized he wasn't cut out for married life. His now *ex*-wife had evidently figured that out, too, since she'd gotten out of Dodge, cheating on him with a colleague.

Emotionally unavailable. Too cold and distant. That's what Theresa had claimed when she confessed she'd fallen in love with someone else. That she wanted a divorce. The sooner, the better.

And she was right. He hadn't been "there" in a very real sense of the word. Oh, he'd loved her in the beginning, but there had been a nagging difficulty in showing that love outside of closed bedroom doors. The same padlock that kept angry emotions imprisoned deep inside of him had evidently trapped the more tender feelings, as well. The strain had taken its toll day by day, and as hurt as he'd been at the time of her confession, he couldn't blame Theresa for looking elsewhere for what she needed.

Hell. Staying a bachelor was the best thing he could do for himself...and for any other woman who might catch his eye. Not that one had. He now knew the stakes and was playing it smarter this time.

A sudden burst of sound from the pipe organ to his right punched through his thoughts, forcing his mind to circle back to what was happening around him. Everyone stood and turned toward the back of the church. And there was Kaleb's bride, her shining eyes fixed on the man beside him. Nicola had her arm through that of an older man, who had to be her father. And in the crook of the man's other arm was his four-month-old granddaughter.

The pounding in his head increased exponentially the closer the entourage got to the front. Right now, all Snow wanted was to get out of the church and head back to the hospital, a world through which he moved with ease. A world he understood and could relate to.

A world that never cheated on him or expected what he couldn't deliver.

He only hoped his friend didn't find out the hard way that marriage was not as easy as the world made it seem.

Although, the fire and passion in Nicola's eyes gave him pause. Evidently Kaleb didn't suck in the emoting department the way Snow did. Then again, Kaleb's childhood and his own had been poles apart.

Maybe, just maybe, this was one marriage

that would survive. One romance that would continue to burn bright.

And if Kaleb found happiness here in this place, who was Snow to question that?

All he knew was that the toast they'd shared at that bar had been just as binding to him as the solemn words his friend was about to exchange with his fiancée.

Till death do us part.

That was a promise Snow was never going to make again. So while Kaleb and Nicola concentrated on their happiness, Snow was going to stand here and mentally renew a different vow. One he'd made years ago, when he was just a child. A vow he'd broken when Theresa had come along.

He was going to stay alone.

The sins of Kaleb's father were not going to be visited upon his son. Not now. Not ever.

Of that, he was sure.

CHAPTER ONE

Three months later

KIRSTEN NADIF WAS LOST.

Damn. She'd been at the hospital for almost a month now, and she still couldn't seem to find her way around some of the floors. NYC Memorial was massive. Her previous hospital, where she'd started her career, was a quarter of the size of this hospital. So it was understandable that she might feel a bit discombobulated.

She laughed. Discombobulated. One of those fun English words she'd learned years ago in her ESL class in Lebanon. She tended to use that word. A lot. Just for that reason. It helped tie her to her roots and reminded her of her purpose for remaining here in

America, even after her father had moved back home.

Not for the first time, she questioned her decision to transfer from Ohio to New York. But it had been for the right reasons. Lately, she'd begun thinking of moving back home to be near her father, and to do that, she would need all the experience she could get. And NYC Memorial was on the cutting edge of pulmonary treatments, including transplantation, a stage her mom had never reached before her death ten years ago. Her dad's decision to move back to Lebanon last year had not been an easy one, and she found she missed him terribly. Never had she felt more alone and out of place than she did right now with people streaming around her.

Just give it time, Kirsten.

She'd already made one friend. Nicola Sabat had seen her wandering down a hallway on her first day at the hospital and had stopped to help, and then invited her to lunch, since she said her husband was at home on "daddy duty"—thanks to a sick babysitter— and Nicola could use the company.

They were on their way to becoming fast friends.

Only today, Nicola was nowhere to be found, and she was late for an appointment with a patient and the hospital's head of transplant surgery.

She spied a sign on the corner of the wide hallway. Critical Care. Finally! Glancing at her cell phone, she saw she was ten minutes late, and now there was a missed-call notification. Her phone had been on silent. Perfect.

Heading in the direction of the arrows, she pressed redial to call the number. It rang once.

"Tangredi."

She blinked at the unfamiliar name before realizing it was the doctor she was supposed to meet. "Hi, this is Dr. Nadif. I'll be there in a minute or two. I got lost. Sorry about that."

There was silence for a few seconds, and Kirsten's chest tightened. Had he hung up on her? She pulled the phone away from her ear to look just as his voice came back through. "Then I guess I'll see you in a minute or two."

Then the phone went dead.

Oh, Lord. Despite the softness of his tone,

she sensed he was irritated. Rightfully so. She should have probably called, but figured the process of finding out how to get in touch with him would make her even more tardy. And she'd had an emergency case in Pediatrics that she'd needed to see to. The ten-year-old had had persistent bronchitis, and after a troubling X-ray she'd ordered an MRI of her lungs that was scheduled for next week. She was probably overreacting, but after her mom…

She shook her head, dropping her cell phone back into her pocket. That was the last thing she needed to think about right now. This was her first time meeting this particular doctor, and their brief interaction on the phone did not bode well for their developing a chummy relationship.

Not that she was looking for "chummy." Or a relationship of any kind, for that matter. Been there, done that and it didn't bear repeating. Then there was the huge move she was contemplating in the next year or two.

She quickened her pace, looking toward the U-shaped bank of white laminated desks, which meant there was a nurses' station just ahead. Faster to ask than to try to find the patient's room on her own.

She approached a male nurse who was standing on the outside of the desk talking to one of the other nurses and stopped. "Excuse me, can either of you tell me where Tanya Latimer's room is?"

The man's head turned toward her, revealing eyes the color of blue, chipped ice. They perched over cheekbones that were just as hard and severe. She suppressed a shiver.

The nurse behind the desk glanced at her lanyard and spoke to the man. "I think this is who you were waiting for, isn't it, Dr. Tangredi?"

Dr. Tangredi.

Ya ilahi! He wasn't a nurse. He was the doctor she was supposed to meet. Having this embarrassing introduction done in front of an audience was not how she'd envisioned this happening. "Oh, um, hello." She stretched out her hand. "I'm Dr. Nadif."

When his skin connected with hers, it was not what she'd expected. At all. Unlike the rest of his forbidding demeanor, his fingers were warm as they curled around hers. Goose bumps—having nothing to do with the overly cool temperature of the hospital—broke out along her arms.

"I know who you are."

That comment startled her before she realized the nurse wasn't the only one who'd glanced at the lanyard hanging at chest level. Swift heat washed into her cheeks, and she wasn't sure why.

"I'm sorry again for being late."

"I let the medical students go on to lunch."

"Medical…oh, right." This was even worse. It hadn't been just the doctor who'd been kept waiting by her lateness—there had also been a group of students. She could explain that she'd had an emergency, and that she hadn't simply been caught up in some romance novel for the last fifteen minutes.

Not that this man knew anything about romance, if the empty ring finger and his chilly tone were anything to go by.

Unfair, Kirsten. He probably has a girlfriend waiting somewhere. After all, he was gorgeous, despite his less than winning personality. She forged on ahead, deciding she was not going to let him intimidate her. "I can always come back, if that's more convenient for you."

"No, the patient is waiting. I'd rather get your assessment now, before we make any other decisions about her treatment."

"Of course." She straightened her back. "Lead the way."

He nodded a goodbye at the nurse behind the desk, and Kirsten threw the woman a quick smile before following Dr. Tangredi down the hallway, catching up to him in a few strides. "So can you tell me a little more about the patient?"

"Tanya Latimer, female, midtwenties. Primary pulmonary hypertension. Her condition degraded until she was placed on the transplant list. Yesterday, she got a new pair of lungs."

He made it sound like something that happened every day. Like you simply went to some parts superstore and picked out what you wanted. In the real world, lungs and livers and hearts were not so easy to come by. It took time—and, often, another family's tragedy—to make it happen.

And that time sometimes ran out before a donor organ became available. She knew that firsthand.

"How's she doing?"

"Blood oxygen is better than it was before the transplant, but not quite where we would like it to be at this point."

"Any signs of rejection?"

His eyes focused on her again. "No. And we're hoping there won't be."

Hoping there wouldn't be signs? Or that the lungs wouldn't be rejected?

The latter, of course.

"Once the inflammation from surgery settles down, that should improve as long as the donor had no underlying health conditions."

"I screened him myself."

Meaning what? That he was infallible? Well, she hated to break it to him, but even the finest doctors in the world couldn't always halt the progression of disease. Her mom was a case in point of that.

"Okay, but I'd like to read your notes, if that's possible, just so I can see if there's…"

She was going to say "to see if there was something you missed," but something stopped her. And that was crazy. Since when had she been afraid to speak her mind? She wasn't. She was just being cautious.

"I'll have them sent to you. But right now I'd like to have you put eyes on her and actually look at her, and not just go by a set of notes or give her a cursory glance."

Kirsten stiffened. She always looked at her patients—*really* looked. Why was she feeling so defensive all of a sudden? Maybe because he'd gotten prickly when she'd questioned him, and now he was doing the same to her.

"That's why I came down here."

They stared at each other for a long moment before Dr. Tangredi did something that shocked her. He smiled. It was a smile that floored her with its sudden infusion of warmth. Even his eyes had been transformed into a deeper hue of blue. She struggled to catch her breath for a moment.

"Call me Snow. Please. Most people do."

It wasn't just the change in his demeanor that threw her, but the abrupt change in topic did, too. She felt… *Don't say it.*

Her mind filled the blank, anyway. She felt discombobulated.

You really are going to have to find a new favorite word.

Snow. Man, the name fit him. But as long he didn't try to launch any more ice spears at her, she could deal with the name.

"I'm Kirsten."

"All right, Kirsten, let's go see our patient, then."

He pushed through the door of the room, and the first thing that met Kirsten's ears was…noise. Lots of it. During her pulmonary workups she was used to listening closely, whether it was to note subtle changes in lung function through her stethoscope, or to ask a patient to blow through a peak-flow meter. She was used to an asthmatic wheeze and other sounds of oxygen being moved, but the cacophony of an ICU room was always startling to her senses. Cardiac monitors beeped and ventilators hissed, along with the sound of other machines.

The patient's eyes were open, watching them. She followed Snow over to the bed.

"Hello, Ms. Latimer, I'm Dr. Nadif. I'm one of Dr. Tangredi's, er, colleagues. I'm a pulmonologist. And I'd like to check to see how you're doing, if that's okay."

The woman nodded. It had to be a frightening experience to not be able to control your respiration, or speak…to be totally at the mercy of the machines and caregivers. A wave of compassion went through her.

Kirsten went over to the dispenser on the wall and sanitized her hands, then snapped on gloves. Next, she took the woman's hand in her own. "Dr. Tangredi is going to help me examine you, but if anything hurts unbearably in the process, I want you to squeeze my hand, okay?"

Another nod.

She glanced at Snow. "Can you put my stethoscope in my ears so I don't contaminate anything? I can't do it one-handed. It's in my pocket."

Snow's head tilted, but he did as she asked, coming closer and sliding his gloved hand into her pocket. A wave of some weird emotion slid over her as his fingers curled around the instrument, sliding across her hip for a second. But before that emotion had fully registered, he'd pulled out her listening device, uncoiled it and stood in front of her to slide the earpieces in place. He was so close, she could smell the light tangy scent of his aftershave. His hands brushed over her cheekbones as he adjusted the fit. For once she was glad for the noise in the room. It would help mask any changes in her own breathing. And she knew there was a change. She could feel it. Feel it in the sudden heat that flared in her face, in the pulse that thumped in her neck.

"Thanks, that's good." She should have tried to do it herself, rather than risking having him come so close. But, after her breakup with Dave, she'd thought she was immune to men, and had no idea she was going to react to Tangredi the way she had.

Fortunately, he moved back several steps, eyes clipping hers, before he glanced again at the patient.

She took a second to compose herself, then addressed Tanya. "I'm going to listen to your lungs. This might be a little chilly." Still holding the woman's hand, she adjusted the hospital gown so that she had enough room. She wouldn't be able to listen through the patient's back unless they sat her upright, and Kirsten didn't want to do that unless absolutely necessary. She was pretty sure they had already moved her around a lot. Tanya didn't need yet another set of hands causing her pain.

Avoiding the drain tubes and the incision down the middle of her chest, she gently placed her stethoscope on the patient's sides and under her collarbone, listening to bronchial sounds and the inflation of the lungs themselves.

She didn't detect any crackling, which was good. The patient's heart sounded good and strong, as well, and the sides of her neck indicated she had good blood flow to the brain. "Everything sounds the way it should. What's your pain level on a scale of one to ten? You can either squeeze my hand that many times or hold up fingers."

There was a pause and then she lifted her other hand and held up four fingers. So her pain level was a four. She glanced at Snow. "Is that what you'd expect at this point? Or does she need something more?"

Snow checked the chart, then looked at Tanya. "You have another dose of meds coming in just a few minutes. Are you okay until then?"

The woman nodded.

"Good," Kirsten said. "It won't be long, okay?" She gently palpated the woman's belly and then let go of her hand in order to move to her ankles. "No peripheral edema that I can see."

"Yes, I noted that, as well."

"I think she looks good. Good color. So my opinion would be to monitor to make sure her oxygen levels don't drop further, and I would expect to see an improvement tomorrow or the next day." She glanced at Tanya. "And some of your pain should start subsiding a bit in a week or so. Once your incision starts to heal, it will go a long way toward making you more comfortable."

Tanya nodded again. Something pulled at her, though. Something in the woman's eyes that made her want to stay here with her. But she couldn't. Kirsten gave her a smile and then checked her IV bags, noting the medications and the drip. "Can I come back to see how you're doing tomorrow?"

The woman seemed to relax into herself, and her eyes closed, almost as if she was relieved. Kirsten had been right. When she looked at Snow, however, he didn't look nearly as pleased. Afraid she was hijacking his patient? Not likely. He was the transplant expert, not her. She just knew lungs. And from the sounds of them working, this woman had gained a good set of them. But there just seemed to be something...more.

Something she couldn't quite put her finger on. Her instincts weren't often wrong.

"Can I see you outside?" Snow smiled at the patient, but the chill was back in his eyes. "I'll check in with you later this afternoon, Ms. Latimer."

Kirsten stripped off her gloves, dropping them into the waste receptacle as she went outside, then coiled her stethoscope again and stuffed it back in her pocket.

Before Snow could lay into her—which is what she suspected he might do—she decided to explain first and leave her uneasy feelings out of the mix, since those were harder to explain. "Seeing her today gave me a baseline of comparison for what's going on. I'd like to check for improvement over the next twenty-four hours in order to predict how she's going to do. That's why you called for the consult, right?"

"Yes. I just didn't realize it would take more than once to satisfy you."

She shot him a glance, then realized he'd meant nothing by those words. It was her own weird reaction to him that was putting thoughts in her head. Time to get back to her reasons for coming to New York. "Is pulse oxygen normally higher than the eighties when you first perform a lung transplant?"

"Pretty much. There's usually a dramatic improvement right away, but considering where most of them start, almost anything is better than where they were before surgery. Over the next couple of days, there should be a steady climb. But these patients are normally in a hypoxic state by the time they're approved for transplantation. And then there's the wait time."

"So why were you concerned with this particular patient?"

He paused before answering. "I've noticed what I think is some apathy, lately, about the process. Transplant candidates go through a rigorous screening process before they're placed on the list. She passed it, but…" He shrugged. "I would say it's a gut feeling more than anything, but my gut's track record has been known to have its weak spots."

She couldn't imagine Snowden Trangredi being anything less than totally self-assured and confident with his decisions. But she guessed anyone could have a bad day and get something wrong. But to admit it? That surprised her, after his attitude earlier.

So what had he been wrong about? A patient? Something else?

"What makes you think she's not fully on board?" She'd had an odd feeling about Tanya, too, so it helped knowing she wasn't the only one.

"Not sure. Like I said, it's just a gut feeling, but she's shown neither excitement nor fear in the hours leading up to surgery. Something just didn't feel right, but since she'd already been approved, it was almost too late to send a concern up the chain to the transplant board. And if I sounded the alarm and was wrong, then a person who desperately needed a transplant might end up overlooked. Or worse, die. And I didn't want that to happen."

Snowden's light hair was just a little too long, the natural curliness very much in evidence at the ends and across the top. It fell down over his forehead in a way that made her tummy heat. And those eyes seemed to see everything. It unnerved her. And it also made her take a mental step back.

Leaning a shoulder against the wall beside her, he glanced at her. "So you've been at NYC Memorial how long now? I know

Dr. Billings retired, but I wasn't sure who'd taken his place."

She'd arrived two days before Billings officially left, so there'd been almost no time for him to show her the ropes. They'd been too busy going over his patient files and explaining the rationale behind his treatment methods. They'd been very different from what she'd done at her former hospital.

"I've been here almost a month. I guess it took them longer than they expected to find someone who was qualified to take Dr. Billings's place, although I'm not quite sure why I beat out the other applicants. So I'd barely skidded in before he left. It left me feeling kind of discombobulated."

He blinked. "Discombobulated."

Too late, she realized she'd actually used the word in a sentence. That's what she got for reciting it in her head one too many times. She rushed to cover her blunder.

"It means—"

"I know what the word means. I just don't think I've ever heard someone say it. Out loud."

One side of his mouth curved up in that same smile he'd given her earlier, and that mental step back she'd taken earlier all but disappeared. The problem was, while his smile relieved one kind of tension, it caused another to sprout up in its place. And this one was a bit wilder, a bit more unpredictable.

She did not need wild and unpredictable. Not at this point in her life.

She cleared her throat. "Well, it's just one of those fun words. It helps me not take myself too seriously. I think the world has a habit of doing just that. Being too serious. Too…distant. We don't make the connections we need to."

Connections? What the hell was she talking about?

Snow must have wondered the same thing because his smile faded, and he seemed to stiffen. "As a doctor, I've found it's better to maintain a certain distance with my patients."

This sounded like an argument he'd had before. The explanation seemed to come too quickly. Maybe she wasn't the only one who'd thought his name fit the man. Except she'd seen a crack or two in icy coating. "Yes, of course."

He shoved back that stray lock of hair, dragging his fingers through it as if making an effort to keep it back.

Was he used to it being shorter? She hoped not. She kind of like it that length. It was the only thing about him that didn't seem to be under some kind of tight control. It was wild and unpredictable.

Ya llahi! The curse rolled through her head as she clamped down on that observation. Those were the exact words she'd come up with moments earlier.

She certainly didn't need to stand here thinking about the length of his hair or how much self-control the man had. "Well, thanks for asking me to come see Ms. Latimer. You're sure you're okay with me coming back tomorrow? I can come while you're doing rounds if you'd prefer."

"Not necessary. And I think she'd like it if you visited again. She seemed to perk up when you stood beside her. Held her hand. I don't usually get that kind of reception during her appointments."

"It's probably a programmed response." She didn't want him to get back on the subject of maintaining a professional distance, since she was having a little trouble doing that with him right now.

"A what?"

She shrugged. "She probably associates you with pain or discomfort…or fear. I'm not there to do a procedure on her, so she doesn't view me as threatening."

"Threatening." The way he said the word was ominous and not at all what she'd meant.

She was digging herself in deeper. Time to back out of the hole. "I don't mean in a physical way. It has nothing to do with you personally, I'm sure. It's kind of like some people being afraid of the dentist. It doesn't matter how nice they are, sometimes it's associated with something unpleasant, even though it's necessary."

"And you're not associated with that."

"Nope. I'm only there to examine. Not to perform any kind of procedure, and subconsciously Tanya knows it."

"Guess I never thought of it like that."

"I'm sure she's grateful for what you're doing." She hesitated. "Would you mind if I tried talking to her about the surgery and what it means for her? Maybe what you're seeing as apathy really is fear."

"Fear. Hell. Not what I wanted." He took a deep breath and blew it back out. "Okay. I want to be kept in the loop, though. So no secrets, even if she asks you not to tell me something. This is her life we're talking about. I don't want there to be any misunderstandings or hiding of information."

That stung. "Of course. I realize she's your patient, not mine. If she says something I think is important, I'll let you know. You have my word."

"Thank you. I appreciate that."

He paused. "Could you give me a call as soon as you see her? I'll schedule her in my afternoon rounds rather than morning, so I can check any areas of concern you may have. My number should be in your phone, since I called you."

"Yes. I'll add you to my contacts." Did she really need to do that? It's not like they were going to work together on a daily basis, but if she didn't, she'd have to guess which one of the numbers was his. *Sure, Kirsten. That's the reason.* She gave an internal eye roll.

"Sounds good." With that he pushed away from the wall and walked down the hallway. It wasn't quite a swagger, but his lithe body had a loose-limbed way of going that made him seem completely at ease with himself. And why wouldn't he be? He had everything in the world going for him. Looks, skill, personality… She paused at that last one. Well, maybe he had a winning personality. If he chose to show that side of himself. She had a feeling he could be a formidable enemy, though, if provoked.

Well then, she would do her best not to provoke him on purpose, but if he got his feathers ruffled over nothing, she was certainly not going to apologize for the sake of mollifying him.

Kirsten was pretty strong-willed herself, so that could go both ways. Hopefully neither of them would see fit to test the other's limits.

Because she was pretty sure neither she nor Snow would like the outcome, if that happened.

CHAPTER TWO

SNOW WAITED MOST of the morning for her call.

It galled him that he had spent more time than he should have sitting in his office, replaying the sound of her voice in his mind. Her slight accent had a different rise and fall than what he was used to hearing. Although in a city the size of New York, he'd heard a lot of different accents. And a lot of intonations. Until she'd used the words *threatening* and *fear* in relation to his patient. And then he'd been transported back to another world, a world where those two words held a very different meaning.

At home as a child, he'd learned to read voices well and knew when it was time to flee the vicinity. There was a certain blurring of words—the way they ran together in a string of nonsensical phrases—that never boded well for those who lived in his household. So he'd normally chosen that time to grab his bike and ride to his friend Kaleb's house.

The only tone in the Sabat household had been calm. Controlled. Snow had internalized those softer voices and magnified them into a type of self-protection that he'd used at home during the worst times. He'd learned it was possible to keep his emotions in check.

At least he hoped he could. He'd been able to do it with Theresa, keeping a big portion of his childhood a secret from her. But if that fail-safe ever came tumbling down?

He'd decided a while back he was never going to let himself get into a situation where he might lose control of his emotions. The divorce had been a godsend, actually. He no longer had to fear losing his temper, never had to feel his way around every discussion looking for a way to keep things from escalating into an outright argument.

He'd heard a hint of irritation in Kirsten's voice at one point of their conversation, but no real anger. No sharp temper that could wound his patients. Instead, he'd been the one who'd gotten a little testy, and he didn't like it. Didn't like that someone he barely knew had been able to get a rise out of him, when Theresa never could.

"Just get angry, Snow!" she'd insisted toward the end. "Don't freeze me out."

She'd never understood that anger was one of those emotions he'd banished from his vocabulary. That had probably been the last real conversation he and his ex had had, before she found what she'd been looking for in someone else's arms.

It had been his fault. He was enough of a realist to admit it. And he'd been reading the signs—just like he had during his childhood—for a long time. He just hadn't been able to, or wanted, to do anything about it. He had not wanted his past to rise up and overwhelm his defenses.

Was that what his dad had felt every time he picked up a bottle? Every time he lifted his hand in anger?

Snow didn't drink much anymore. He could remember a couple of times he'd gotten roaring drunk as a way to escape. One of those time was when he'd gone to the bar with Kaleb to celebrate his divorce.

And once when he'd realized his good friend might have found what Snow hadn't been able to find: love. He wasn't an alcoholic, like his dad, but he'd decided about six months ago that he was done with the stuff—a twinge of fear that there might be a genetic component to his dad's problems that might eventually catch up to him.

That's probably why Kirsten's offhand comment had burrowed deep and stayed there.

He glanced at the phone on his desk. Damn. Time to get up and get some work done. He'd told Kirsten he would check on their patient later this afternoon, but maybe he would go early. Wait. *Their* patient? He'd used that term yesterday, too, when talking to Kirsten.

His jaw clenched. Tanya Latimer was *his* patient. He'd done the surgery. He'd done the lead-up. Ultimately, what happened to her was on him. There would be no one to swoop in and rescue her if he wasn't on his toes. Just like there'd been no one to swoop in and rescue him and his mom.

Just as he pried himself out of his chair, the desk phone went off. His nerves immediately kicked into high gear. He took a moment to calm himself before picking it up. Despite his efforts, he practically growled a greeting before catching himself.

Hell, what was wrong with him?

"Dr. Tangredi—Snow?"

"Yes." He recognized her voice immediately, sinking back into his chair. "How is she?"

No asking her how she was or how her day was going. He was turning into a first-class jerk.

"I did talk to her." There was a long pause. "Could we, er, meet somewhere to discuss it? I feel like this is better said in person than over the phone."

A sense of foreboding went through him. Maybe Tanya had decided she wanted to stop the process or get a new doctor. Hell, if that happened he was not going to be happy. Not with his patient and not with himself, for ignoring his gut.

"Is now a good time? I can meet you here in my office, or in the staff lounge, whichever is better."

Another pause. "I did get permission to share what's going on with you, but just barely. I think it might be better done in a private place to respect her wishes."

A private place. He liked the tiny differences in the way she phrased things. Like when she'd used the word *discombobulated*. It was unique to her, and…

Damn attractive.

Except he didn't need to find anything about her attractive. Not her raven-colored locks. Not the blue eyes that were such a contrast to her skin tone. "How about here in my office, then?"

That was about as private as it got.

"Okay. Which number?"

"Four-oh-three."

"I'll be up there in a few minutes."

For a split second he wondered if it would have been better to go somewhere for coffee outside of the hospital. He could have found someplace where they would be unlikely to run across anyone he knew. There were other ways to assure privacy without it needing to be a place where it was only the two of them.

Too late now. He'd already invited her up.

He straightened his desk, then got up and moved over to a small seating arrangement in the far corner, consisting of a leather sofa and two matching chairs. He stopped himself. It didn't matter what the space looked like. He wasn't entertaining her. He was having a professional discussion.

Still, he closed the door to the bathroom across from the chairs.

Just as he did, there was a knock on his door. She'd been close. Maybe she was coming from her own office, since they were all on the fourth floor.

He went behind his desk and sat down. "Come in."

Kirsten poked her head in as if to assure herself that she had the right office, then entered the room, shutting the door quietly behind herself. "Hi. Thanks for seeing me." She glanced at his door, her head tilting.

"I wondered if you'd forgotten about calling me this morning." Damn. If that didn't sound like he was sitting here wringing his hands as he waited for her call, he didn't know what did.

She lowered herself into a chair and glanced again at his door. "Is there something I should know about the hospital?"

He blinked. Was she worried about being

alone with him? That thought gutted him. "Such as…?"

"You have an extra lock on your door. Mine only has the one on the doorknob."

He stiffened, even as a wave of relief went through him. It was the door she was worried about, not him. And she was right. He'd had a dead bolt installed. Another habit that he hadn't been able to break. But this one was harmless. "No, there's nothing other than the fact that we're in a big city."

"Do I need more locks?"

Hell, he hoped not. "It was an option when I started at the hospital. You have to do what you feel most comfortable with." It hadn't actually been an option, but they'd asked him if he needed anything specific in his office, and he'd asked about the extra lock, since he did periodically sleep on the couch when he had an especially critical patient. "I sometimes have to spend the night here."

She nodded. "Ah, okay, I see."

He had a feeling she didn't really, but this was one subject he didn't want to dwell on or pick apart. "You didn't come here to discuss the lock on my door, though."

"No." She leaned forward. "Did you ever talk to your patient about her future plans?"

He went back through the various conversations he'd had with her, her husband and her parents. "She was pretty ill by the time I met her. She was in the last stages of primary pulmonary hypertension and if she didn't have a transplant, she would die. Her heart was already enlarged and threatening to fail. They all said transplantation was what she wanted. Including Tanya." He was explaining a lot more than he needed to. Maybe because he wasn't sure what Kirsten was getting at. Could he have missed a concern during one of their conversations? Was she planning on doing something else that required a pristine set of lungs? "If there was a concern, she should have discussed it before agreeing to the transplant."

"It has nothing to do with the transplant. Well, it does, but only indirectly."

"What is it, then?"

"It has to do with her antirejection meds."

He leaned back in his chair, dragging his hand through his hair, his fingers snarling in it for a second. He needed to get the damn curls cut off. He made sure his voice was very steady when he said, "Not taking them is not an option. It will *never* be an option. She knew that up front. It's a lifetime commitment. If there are problems with cost or insurance coverage, we can work through them, and the hospital has a program that—"

"It's not the cost. At least that's not what she relayed to me."

She shifted in her chair as if dreading whatever it was the patient had told her. He probably wasn't helping by reacting every time she said something. Sure, he hadn't raised his voice and his tone had been low, soft even, but maybe she was just as good at reading undertones as he was. Because what he was reading from her was off the chart. There was empathy, a trace of pity. And impatience. He was pretty sure that was directed at him.

Well, he was getting pretty damn impatient himself, despite his efforts to the contrary. "I'm waiting for you to tell me what the problem is. That was our agreement. That you not withhold information."

The way he'd withheld information from Theresa? Information he should have trusted her with. No, that was completely different from this situation.

"I know." Her voice was softer than his had been. "What are the effects of her medication on…fertility? Especially the teratogenic properties."

It came to him in a flash. Tanya was a young woman in her midtwenties. They'd asked the standard questions and taken blood test after blood test, checking for levels of certain things as well as pregnancy before the transplant and the steps leading up to it.

"She can't get pregnant." He qualified that. "She *shouldn't* get pregnant. Not right now."

"Then there you have it. If you want to know what's wrong and why she seems worried or upset. That's it in a—" she paused as if looking for the right word "—nutshell."

That made him smile, erasing his earlier thoughts about his childhood. "I see. So like I said, she shouldn't get pregnant right now. But that doesn't mean that she'll never be able to carry a child to term. But there are risks that come with pregnancy. And she needs to wait. She's on the largest doses of immunosuppressants right now, when the risk for rejection is at its highest. But we'll gradually wean her from some of those as her condition becomes more stable."

"So there's still a chance she could have children."

"Yes. But it won't be easy, and she can't just suddenly decide to get pregnant. It will have to be well-planned so we can juggle her medications and monitor her. Some of them have deleterious effects on pregnancy and on the fetus itself."

"That is very good news. Not the deleterious part—that means harmful, right?—but the fact that it can be done. I knew in general it was possible—after all there have been uterine transplants done—but I didn't know in this specific case..." She paused. "It took a long time for her to be willing to tell me this. She had to write it all down, since she's still on the ventilator, and she was visibly upset as she wrote."

He could relate to that. It would be a long time—if ever—before he felt comfortable enough with anyone to share certain things. And yet Kirsten had gained his patient's trust in, what...? Less than three hours?

He was going to need to watch his step around her.

Kirsten pulled a piece of paper from her pocket and opened it to show him what Tanya had written. The ink was smeared in places, like something wet had dripped on it. He glanced at her.

"She was crying."

His gut contracted into a tight ball. "Damn. Why didn't she ask me this before the procedure? I could have put her mind at ease."

"She was worried about dying before the procedure. Her survival instincts were hoping for a way out. An escape. And when the possibility of a transplant was placed on the table, she grabbed at it. Only now is she able to think beyond that, to the consequences of her decision."

He could relate to that all too well. At one time, Snow's survival instincts had given him a blatant disregard for anyone's well-being outside of his own. Empathy had been a hard commodity to find. It was there. Just submerged under the junk that littered his life.

His mom and Kaleb were two of the few

people he cared about. Two of the few people he trusted. And now his mom was finally out of harm's way. His dad had put her in ICU for weeks. When she'd recovered and found he'd been arrested for what he'd done, she finally divorced his ass. Snow hadn't been in contact with the scumbag in over the decade he'd been behind bars. His mom had undergone counseling. And Snow? Well he'd been self-sufficient for a very long time. Counseling wouldn't help whatever was left of the damage his father had inflicted. And maybe that was for the best. It served as a reminder—a kind of cautionary tale.

"They're not permanent consequences. Maybe in a year we can start thinking in terms of having children." Too late, he realized his last phrase could have been construed differently from the way he'd meant it. "Tanya and her husband I mean."

She grinned, a cute dimple forming in her right cheek. "I knew what you meant. Us having children? That would be a very bad match, I think. Besides, who knows where I'll be in a year's time."

He got hung up for a second on her saying they would be a very bad match, before moving to the last sentence.

"Are you thinking of leaving NYC Memorial already?"

"No. Not yet. We just never know where life will take us."

She was avoiding answering him directly. Maybe another hospital was wooing her. Or maybe she just wasn't happy here. Well, it was none of his business. If she left tomorrow, life as he knew it would simply go on unaltered. Except didn't he owe it to the hospital to be a positive force and not a negative one that created a toxic workplace? Maybe he should make more of an effort to be conciliatory and friendly—find a little of that misplaced empathy and put it on display.

"I do appreciate your help with Tanya. I'll talk to her about the having-children issue." He glanced again at the tearstained paper his patient had written on.

"Do you mind if I talk to her instead? It might be easier coming from me, since she and I have already spoken about it. If you can explain the steps she'll need to take, I'll make sure she knows."

That was fair. After all, Tanya had confided in Kirsten and not in him. And he knew himself well enough to realize that the pulmonologist presented a much more sympathetic face than he did. Snow was driven from task to task, moving to the beat of mental checklists that needed to be completed each day. Feelings—and talking about them—didn't come easily for him. He shied away from them both with patients and in his personal life. But he had a feeling that Kirsten had no such problems. Neither had Theresa. She'd put in a whole lot more than she'd gotten out of their marriage. It's why, in the end, she'd decided he wasn't worth the effort. And he couldn't blame her.

Oh, he could for the affair. She should have just asked for a divorce and been done with it. She certainly had once she'd found someone else.

But he and Kirsten were colleagues and nothing else. So there was no need to worry about that kind of incompatibility. As long as his transplant patient was on the road to recovery, that's what he needed to focus on. That, and nothing else.

So as long as this particular problem was on its way to being solved, he could go back to what he did best. Treat his patient's physical needs while leaving the emotional side to someone else.

Someone other than him.

The cell phone that had been on his desk buzzed. He glanced at the screen. "Sorry, I need to take this."

"Okay, I'll talk to you later, then."

He nodded, picked up the phone and barked out his name. He listened for a second to the doctor in the emergency room, then stuck his head out of the door, catching Kirsten before she'd gotten halfway down the hall.

"Hey, Kirsten, could you hold up for a second?"

She turned with a frown, then headed back toward him.

His attention went back to the doctor. "I'll be right down. I'll have our new pulmonologist with me."

At least he hoped he would. Maybe she had another patient scheduled.

He hung up. "There's a case down in the ER. A lung-transplant patient from another state was visiting relatives here when he started having trouble breathing. Do you have time to go see him with me?"

"Yes, of course. Do you know anything else?"

They stood in front of the elevators. "Male in his thirties. Pulse ox isn't great, and it looks almost like a virus is attacking his lungs. At least that's what they're guessing. They want me down there in case it's the beginning of organ rejection."

They got on and Snow pushed the button for the first floor.

"And me?"

"I'd like another set of eyes and ears. Treating someone else's patient isn't the easiest."

Her eyebrows went up. "Or dealing with the doctors who treated them."

That got a smile out of him. "Are you thinking of any doctor in particular?"

Her eyes rounded as if in mock surprise. "Of course not. I don't ever have run-ins with other patients' doctors."

He laughed. "Somehow, I don't think that's true."

They came out on the first floor and he headed toward the emergency department with Kirsten close behind. The nurse at reception, a phone to her ear, pointed toward the first exam room on the left. One of the trauma rooms.

Snow pushed through the doors and found Dr. Lawrence standing next to a patient who had an oxygen mask over his face. "Thanks for coming. This is Randy Stewart. He came to visit his parents for a couple of days and started to feel a tightness in his chest."

Snow came over and greeted the patient. "Hi, Randy. I'm Snowden Tangredi, head of transplant surgery here at the hospital. Dr. Nadir is a lung specialist. So you're having a little trouble breathing, Randy?"

He nodded, breath coming out on an extended wheeze. A sound Snow did not like. "Just in the last two hours."

"Okay. I know Dr. Lawrence has already listened to your lungs, but I'm going to take another quick listen, okay?"

Using his stethoscope, he listened to the sounds coming from his lungs, frowning as he thought he picked up a slight sound almost like...

He motioned Kirsten over. "Can you listen for a minute and tell me what you think?"

Kirsten followed his lead and leaned in close, her eyes closed in concentration.

Snow studied her. Although he hadn't actually worked a case with her, other than Tanya's, he got the sense that she was nothing if not thorough. She'd gotten to the heart of the issue with Tanya, hadn't she?

It was one of the reasons he'd wanted her to come with him.

Her eyes popped open, finding his immediately. "I'm hearing some crackling."

"Yeah, me, too." He glanced at Dr. Lawrence, who nodded. "I did, too. If he wasn't a transplant patient, I'd say he was having an asthma attack."

Kirsten spoke up. "I agree. My asthmatic patients have this exact same sound."

What were the odds?

"Did you get ahold of Randy's transplant surgeon?"

"No, he's on vacation in the Bahamas. But they're accessing his records for us."

Randy lowered the mask for a second. "I had a checkup a month ago with my surgeon and everything was fine then."

"So you've had no problems before coming here for vacation."

"None."

"Where is home for you?"

"Montana." He wheezed again, but the sound wasn't quite as labored as his last breath had been.

Kirsten came up beside him. "Montana probably doesn't have the allergens there that we have here."

The pollution index had been high for the last week.

He sat on the stool and pulled over to the bed. "Did your doctor mention anything about the donor lungs? Any diagnosed problems?"

"No. The person had a traumatic brain injury from a traffic accident. Nothing involving the lungs at all. He was young, in his teens." Randy swallowed before reaching above the oxygen mask to pinch the bridge of his nose, as if fighting emotion.

He could very well feel conflicted. It was always hard discussing the donor. Transplant patients were always aware that their salvation came at the death of someone else. It was hard.

Kirsten came over and put her hand on his

arm. "That teenager gave you a gift of life. I'm sure he would be happy to know that."

Even as he watched, the patient's hand dropped back to his side. "Thank you."

Kirsten had something that Snow didn't—that ability to somehow connect with a patient on an emotional level and reassure them. She'd done it with Tanya, when he hadn't been able to. Just another sign that he lacked some sort of empathy gene. Nature? Or nurture?

Hell, did it even matter? His dad had taken something more than Snow's ability to trust people with his deepest emotions. He had also screwed up his ability to relate to people in a visceral, instinctive way. Maybe partly because he didn't trust people enough to show vulnerability.

It made him good at being objective, gave him the means to look at things through a lens of science rather than a lens of feelings.

But Kirsten could go so far beyond that. And a part of him wished he could somehow tap that part of himself.

He couldn't, though. And that was all there was to it. He was also going to need to be careful around Kirsten. If she had a gift for unearthing emotions in others, might she somehow be able to dig beneath the rubble inside of him and find something he didn't want found?

Hell, he hoped not.

A nurse stuck her head in and handed him a tablet. "They just sent over the records from Montana."

"Great, thanks."

"And, Dr. Lawrence, I have a patient out front who's complaining of chest pains."

"I'll be right there." The other doctor threw him an apologetic look. "Can you take it from here?"

"Yep. We've got it."

We. Meaning him and Kirsten.

Well, he was the one who'd asked her to come. And it had been the right decision, despite the little part inside of him that warned him to keep his distance.

He flipped through the tablet, catching bits and phrases and sorting them into slots in his brain. Randy was right. There was no mention of asthma in the donor. But that didn't mean that it wasn't there. If he was a teen, he could have wheezed from time to time, but not enough to lead to a diagnosis. And the donor was also from Montana.

Setting down the tablet, he waited for Kirsten to finish saying something to the patient. Something that actually made the man laugh. He frowned, a spike of something going through him. Was he jealous? Jealous of her ability to be at ease around someone she barely knew?

Of course not.

He moved closer, waiting for Kirsten to look at him. "I'd like to run a test or two and if those show what I think they might, I want to give you a breathing treatment."

"So it's not rejection?" Randy's voice held a hint of fear.

"I don't think so."

"Thank God. I told my wife to stay at home with the kids. I haven't even called her to let her know I'm at the hospital. This was just going to be a quick trip to help my parents sort out the details of their wills." He paused. "I'm a lawyer, so I don't want to leave that kind of thing with just anyone."

"I can understand that." Just like Snow didn't want to leave the details of his past with just anyone.

Kirsten glanced at him. "So you *are* thinking asthma attack?"

"I do. Your thoughts?"

"The same. He said the tightness is easing a bit."

"Good news." Snow forced a smile. "So let's get you patched up and out of here. Unless you want to stick around for a while longer?"

Randy laughed. "No. I've seen just about all I want to see of hospitals."

"I can imagine. So while we want you to explore some of New York, a tour of the hospital isn't on most of the popular sightseeing routes."

"I'm okay to fly out day after tomorrow?"

"If this is what I think it is, then yes. But I do want you to follow up with your doctor at home. Sooner rather than later. They'll probably want to add a rescue inhaler to your regimen, although I hope this never happens again."

"I don't know how to thank you."

This time, Snow's smile wasn't forced. "Just live your best life and enjoy every breath."

"Thank you. I intend to do exactly that."

* * *

Kirsten should have felt better after her talk with Snow. Especially after treating Randy Stewart with him. The transplant surgeon had gotten the diagnosis exactly right. She should feel gratified that they'd been on the same page, and how easy it had been to treat that patient...together.

But as she walked from her office toward the elevator a half hour later, she was left with a nagging sense of unease. It wasn't due to the patient. It was the extra lock on the door to Snow's office. She'd made it a point to glance at the other office doors on the way back to her own office after the emergency case. No one else had anything marring the wood of their doors. His excuse had been that he sometimes slept in his office. But surely other doctors did, as well. Did he really expect someone to break in and disturb his sleep?

A chill went over her. Maybe he needed the extra lock for a completely different reason. Like not getting caught doing something he shouldn't.

Stop it, Kirsten. The man is not a drug addict.

Nothing in his demeanor indicated anything of the sort. He'd been completely lucid every time she'd seen him. But how many times had doctors hidden such habits?

Well, she didn't personally know any, but she'd heard the stories. And had been warned countless times in medical school not to start down that path.

She'd just pushed the call button for the elevator and gotten on when a hand stopped it from closing. Snow stood in the doorway looking more than a little bit intimidating. As if he'd heard her thoughts and knew exactly where to find her.

Ridiculous.

"I'm headed to lunch. Care to join me?" He stepped into the elevator and pushed the button for the ground floor.

She blinked. The difference between the Snow in his office and the one asking her to lunch seemed almost night and day. "Are you going somewhere close? I need to be back in an hour."

"There's a bistro that serves soup and sandwiches right around the corner—Sergio's. Have you ever been there?"

She hadn't been to very many restaurants, since she was still getting to know people, and she hated to eat at a restaurant alone. Lots of people did it, and she wasn't sure why she was so opposed to doing the same, but it made her feel even more isolated. Maybe she was just missing her dad. Or her former hospital. Whatever it was, the prospect of sitting down to a meal with another person was very appealing. Even if she hadn't gotten off to a very good start with the man who'd invited her.

"I haven't, but I would love to try it."

"Okay. And I promise not to talk shop."

"Shop?"

"To talk about work and patients."

Well, she couldn't imagine what else they would have to talk about. "It's okay. I find work interesting. And I bet you've had some fascinating cases."

"I'm sure you've had your share, as well." He smiled. "But my stomach has been yelling at me for an hour. And I realize that I'm not the most friendly member of NYC Memorial's staff. I wouldn't want to be the reason you're thinking of leaving."

Thinking of leaving… Oh, what she'd said in his office about not knowing where she'd be in a year. So that's why he was inviting her to lunch. Great.

"Oh. Like I said, I'm not thinking of leaving right now. But if I were, it wouldn't be because of you or anyone else. It would be because it's what I feel I should do. So no need to invite me to lunch if that's what you're worried about. I'm a tough girl. I can handle doctors who 'aren't the most friendly.'"

He gave her a smile. One that carried at least a hint of sincerity. "It's not the only reason I asked you. It's later than I expected, and you've been a big help with Tanya, not to mention Randy. Her writing that list had to have taken up a lot of your time. I thought it might have been a simple thing, like the fear of organ rejection and not wanting to get her hopes up."

The elevator stopped, letting them off. "I was happy to be there for her. And for Randy. But I think Tanya realizing she might just have a future in front of her is what brought on the topic of children. She's finally able to look toward something not related to her illness."

"I guess I should be glad of that then.

We'll hopefully get her weaned off the vent in another day or so."

She remembered something else. "I forgot to mention. Her pulse ox is actually up by another percentage point. So I think you can stop worrying on that front. They're also slowly reducing the settings on her vent, like you'd asked them to do, without any negative effects."

"That is very good news."

Maybe having lunch with him wasn't such a bad idea. It would give her a chance to see what he was like when he wasn't at work. And help her understand the need for the locks.

He's not a drug addict.

The repeated thought almost made her laugh. Since when had she become so suspicious?

They walked through the front lobby of the hospital, the ceiling there stretching up four floors. There were railings and chair groupings on each floor where people could look over the foyer, and a huge chandelier that rivaled the ones found in exclusive hotels. NYC Memorial was a beautiful hospital, she had to admit. Prestigious and influential. She didn't care about the prestige, though. She only cared about what was under its beautiful facade.

Kind of like she cared only about what was beneath Snow's attractive exterior. He seemed to genuinely care about his patients. And his instinct about there being something going on with Tanya had been right on target. So he was insightful. A very good trait in a doctor. Not all of them had it. A lot of times they were so focused on the physical signs of illness that they neglected digging deeper. But Snow had not needed to dig. He'd known something was wrong.

Not something she'd expect if his focus was anywhere other than his patients. That alone made her relax.

And she suddenly realized she was hungry, as well, as her stomach let out a loud burbling sound. Her eyes widened and she gave a little laugh when he glanced at her with raised eyebrows. "Okay, my stomach thinks this is a good idea, too."

"Glad to know I'm not the only one." He nodded at the traffic light in front of them. "We'll turn right here and then the bistro is two buildings down."

They were there in less than two minutes. There was no line of customers that she could see. At least not outside. Well, it was almost one thirty.

It had been just before twelve when she'd called him, and she'd actually been surprised he wasn't already out to lunch. She could have called his cell phone, but something inside had urged her to take the less personal route. Especially after his earlier comment about keeping his distance with patients. Besides, if he'd been out to lunch with someone, she hadn't wanted to disturb him. But, of course, then they'd gotten caught taking care of the transplant patient down in the ER. That had taken an hour in and of itself.

"Well, thanks for inviting me."

"It's fine. I could have eaten in my office or at the hospital cafeteria. I've just done that a lot lately and going off-site today was appealing."

"For me, too." She didn't add that since arriving, she'd been picking up food from the cafeteria and going back to her office with it, just so she wasn't sitting alone at a table.

Well, today she wouldn't be alone. And it

would be the first time she'd gotten to eat at one of the local places.

They were greeted almost immediately and escorted back to a dim booth near the rear of the restaurant. The booth sported high backs topped with frosted glass partitions, giving the space an intimate feel. Maybe she'd spoken too soon about being glad to be off-site. But this was lunch between colleagues. It wasn't a date. So no need to feel awkward about it.

One of the waitstaff came over and greeted them. "What can I get you to drink? We have beer, wine, soft drinks and several types of lemonade."

She wanted a glass of wine, but since she was still working, decided against it. "I'd just like a cup of hot tea, if you have it, and a glass of water."

Snow added, "And I'll have a cola, brand doesn't matter."

"Great. I'll be right back with your drinks."

As soon as she left, Snow asked how she was settling in at the hospital.

"Okay, I think. It's much bigger than what I came from, so it's still a little overwhelming. As you could tell from my getting lost. Dr. Sabat has been a big help, and we've eaten a couple of meals together."

"Dr. Sabat?" He had a weird look on his face. "Kaleb is a nice guy, but—"

"Oh!" She realized what he must think. "No, I meant I've eaten with his wife, Nicola."

He seemed to relax back in his seat. "I keep forgetting that Nicola's last name has changed. They're both great people, and Kaleb and I go way back."

"From what Nicola says, they're head over heels in love. And they sure love that baby."

"Yes, I would say so, although I don't see as much of Kaleb as I used to."

"You said you go way back. Did you know each other in medical school?"

"Try elementary school in upstate New York." He smiled.

That surprised her. Somehow she couldn't picture him as a kid riding his bike with friends. "Wow, and you both ended up being doctors at the same hospital?"

He nodded. "Strange how life works. He was definitely a godsend when… Well, let's just say he was there at a time when I really needed a friend."

That touched her, and she wasn't sure why. He'd said Kaleb was a godsend when he needed a friend. So there'd been a rocky period in his life? It certainly sounded like it. That lock on his door crossed her mind's eye before she dismissed it.

She tried to think of a subtle way to get him to say more as he continued to talk. "So are your parents in the area?" he asked.

"No. My father moved back to Lebanon not too long ago. And my mom passed away ten years ago."

"I'm sorry, Kirsten."

The words were accompanied by a frown, as if he really was sorry. "It's okay. She could have used your skills back when we came to the States looking for a cure, though."

"A cure?"

"She was in the late stages of cystic fibrosis. She'd always said I was her miracle child, since she'd been advised not to get pregnant. I was an accident, but she said she felt like there was a reason for it. So it really made me feel for Tanya."

The waitress came back for their order.

All she wanted was soup and half a sandwich, so she chose the chicken salad and potato soup. Snow opted for a turkey club sandwich.

"Your mom came over here for treatment?"

"A transplant, actually. But she didn't make the list in time. She died a year after we arrived. My dad decided we would stay, since I wanted to go through medical school. I did, and here I am."

"I'm sorry your mom didn't get what she needed." He glanced at her. "You're a pulmonologist..."

She answered his unspoken question. "Yes, my mom is why I went into this specialty. I'd like to think she would have approved."

"I'm sure she would have. She'd have really liked the way you helped Tanya."

"I didn't do much. Just listened." His words warmed her. Did he like the way she'd handled Randy, as well?

"It sounds like that's what she needed the most."

She smiled. "Don't we all, from time to time? Need someone to listen?"

Before he could answer, the waitress chose that moment to come by with their food. She placed their meals in front of them and asked if there was anything else either of them needed, then she slid into the background once again.

"So where did you live before moving to NYC Memorial?"

"I worked at a small hospital in Ohio. My mom was treated at one of the major hospitals there."

He nodded. "And you didn't want to work at the hospital where she was treated?"

"There weren't any open positions in pulmonology there when I started looking. But NYC Memorial had one. And it's okay. I think I needed a change of scenery, anyway. Once my dad moved…well, there was nothing keeping me anchored in Ohio. I thought maybe in a big city, I wouldn't be quite as… tied to needing a car for transportation."

She'd been going to say she wouldn't be as lonely—wouldn't have constant reminders of having her heart broken, of her boyfriend scooting out of her life as if she'd meant nothing at all—but she changed the wording at the last second. He didn't need to know that her immersion in her work was due to a failed relationship. Or that it was on purpose.

At thirty-two she'd only had one serious boyfriend and that was in medical school, where the pressures of studying and internship had taken a toll on them as a couple. She'd needed more from him in terms of emotional support and encouragement, whereas he seemed to handle the later parts of school by becoming laser-focused on the tasks in front of him. It had left her feeling wobbly and insecure. When she tried to talk to him about it, he sidestepped the subject time and time again.

And then, when they'd gone to separate hospitals, he'd walked away from her without so much as a backward glance. It had been a crushing blow. She'd tried texting him occasionally, and while he hadn't exactly ghosted her, his obvious indifference had made the wound fester until she finally deleted his number from her phone.

She decided she wasn't going to give another man the opportunity to turn his back on her like that. It made her decision to return to Lebanon that much easier.

But she had to admit that it was sometimes hard going home to an empty apartment, although she now valued her solitude, for the most part. But she did miss the camaraderie that medical school and the small hospital in Ohio had offered.

"Do you find you miss Lebanon? You said your dad went back there."

This is where it got tricky. She really didn't want anyone to know at this point that she was seriously thinking of going back there. She wasn't certain about it, but it had been rolling around in her mind for a while. What she didn't want to do was sink her chances at NYC Memorial by making that declaration to anyone. Because she might just end up at the hospital for a while.

"I do miss it. I grew up there and almost all of my relatives are there, except for a couple of third cousins who are in Philadelphia." Cousins she'd never met and probably never would. But her dad had made it a point to let her know their names and contact information in case she got into trouble. Not that she would call them.

"I imagine it's hard being away from them."

"Yes. But I love it in New York, as well. And I'm sure this will become 'home' with a little time and a couple more friends."

"Let me know if you need a tour guide for seeing the sights. I know a good one who's lived in New York his whole life."

She hadn't yet ventured into the touristy parts of the city, for the main reason that she'd hit the ground running as soon as she'd arrived. "That would be great. Could you give me the person's contact information?"

"You already have it." He gave her a smile.

She did? She didn't remember seeing that. Was it in the welcome packet or something? "I haven't looked through everything the hospital gave me yet, so I may have overlooked it."

"Actually, it's me. It's the least I can do for helping me out with Tanya. And for how unwelcoming I was when I called looking for you."

She frowned. "I talked to Tanya because I wanted to. And I was late, so I understand why you might have been irritated."

"That may be, but you're new here, and I was kind of rude. We can coordinate our next days off together and spend a morning or afternoon just hitting the high points. If you're okay with doing that."

There was something in his voice that sounded a little uncertain, as if he might think she really had a problem going with him. And, in reality, she might, given some of the tangled emotions he engendered in her, but what could she say? That she didn't want to see New York? Or that she didn't particularly want him as a tour guide? Because honestly, the thought of going from place to place with him held an odd appeal. She'd seen rare glimpses of a softer side of Snow and wondered what he might be like away from the hospital. Those imaginings worried her. Made her consider turning him down.

But going to see those sights on her own seemed almost as sad as sitting in a restaurant by herself. She could ask Nicola to go with her, but she had the baby and not a whole lot of free time, by her own admission.

So she let out a breath and decided to commit herself, before she could chicken out. But only for a day, in case it went horribly wrong. And it very well could. Except this wasn't a relationship or even a date, so what could it hurt?

"Okay. I'll take you up on your offer. Let me know when is good for you, and I'll try to sync my schedule with it."

Even as she said the words she hoped she wasn't making a huge mistake. One that could create problems with him in the future or with the hospital in general. But how could it? One afternoon did not a career break. Or a relationship make.

At least she hoped not.

CHAPTER THREE

HE WAS HAVING SECOND THOUGHTS.

Not about Tanya, whose demeanor had totally changed. She was throwing all of her energy into wanting to rid herself of the ventilator and seemed much more eager to start physical therapy, both of which were supposed to happen tomorrow. He had Kirsten to thank for that. Which is why he'd offered to show her the sights.

Right? The words at the restaurant two days ago had come out of nowhere. But when he'd asked her if she missed Lebanon, she'd gotten this funny look on her face and hadn't quite met his eyes. Was she that homesick? Homesick enough to leave NYC Memorial?

Why wouldn't she be? She'd said her family was all there. Snow didn't understand that kind of homesickness, since his family was at best dysfunctional, and at worst... Well, it's why he liked to lock his doors at night. His father had been out of the picture for a long time, but the habits he'd picked up from his time at home were not.

It's a compulsion. The words whispered through his head, and he was quick to push them back out again. So what if he liked to lock his doors at night? So what if he'd asked for an extra lock on his office at the hospital? That didn't make it a compulsion. But he remembered his mom's hands shaking as she'd struggled to install a lock on Snow's bedroom door after a particularly bad night. He'd been seven at the time, and he hadn't quite understood why one of his mom's eyes was darker than the other. He'd learned soon enough, though, that even brand-new locks didn't always keep monsters at bay.

Hell! He hadn't thought about this in forever. Why now? Maybe it was Kirsten asking about the lock on his office door and frowning as she asked him if she needed one, too. He hoped she never did. Hoped she always felt safe.

Was that why he'd asked if he could show her some sights? Because he'd feel safer if she had someone with her, since she'd shared that she didn't know very many people at the hospital yet?

Ha! How funny was it that he, of all people, thought he could make her feel safe? He was never really sure if his dad's darkness was somehow inside of him. After all, his mom said that he'd been different when they'd first met. That he'd been charming and kind.

Well, Snow was pretty sure he couldn't be accused of being either of those things. But the other?

Damn. Well, he'd make sure she didn't get any funny ideas, not that she'd shown any interest in him. But he also remembered the shock he'd felt when she said that she'd eaten with "Dr. Sabat," and he'd thought she meant Kaleb at first. He knew his friend would never cheat on Nicola, so why had that weird feeling slithered through his gut, coiling there as if waiting to strike if his friend made one wrong move. Was it that darkness he worried about? Or simply because he'd been cheated on before? Just because Theresa had cheated, it didn't mean everyone did.

But Kirsten hadn't mentioned whether or not she was seeing anyone back at her old hospital or not. If she was, surely she wouldn't have agreed to go with him. Right?

Way to show your ignorance, Snow. Women and men can be friends.

With that thought, he went to see his next patient, making a note to himself to call Kirsten and let her know that he had next Wednesday off. If that didn't work, then maybe he could take a portion of one of his personal days and take her around then.

His phone buzzed and he glanced at the readout. He frowned at the coincidence that found his mind on Kirsten at the very moment she was calling him. "Hello? Snow here."

"Um, hi. I'm just checking to see how things with Tanya went today."

He stopped at a nearby waiting area and dropped into a chair, so he didn't have to walk and try to schedule things at the same time. "They went well. Really well. Thanks to you."

"Oh, I'm pretty sure she would have eventually gotten with the program with or without my help. She was just going through a momentary, er, *alhuzin*… How do you say it? A momentary depression, maybe?"

The ease with which that word in her native tongue slid out made him picture her in his mind. Were her straight black locks flowing over her shoulders before being caught in a ponytail partway down its length? Or was her hair loose and free, allowing him to…? Something shifted in his gut, and this time it wasn't a slithery dark sensation. But it was just as dangerous. And he needed to take it seriously.

"Yes, a momentary depression is the perfect word to describe it. But she seems to be looking forward to recovering now."

"And maybe having a baby of her own?"

"Yes. Maybe. We're certainly not ruling anything out at the moment."

"So, since Tanya is doing well, maybe I can ask your opinion on a patient of my own? She's a ten-year-old girl."

Ah, so this was the reason for her call, although he was pretty sure her interest in how Tanya was doing was genuine. "Of course. Is she in the hospital?"

"Not at the moment, but today was my second time seeing her over the period of a week. I'm suspecting something more is going on besides a chest infection. She's short of breath, even though I don't see any signs of bacterial pneumonia or a viral infection."

"That's a positive."

There was a pause. "It is, although ruling out simple reasons makes me suspect it might be a more complicated condition."

"Such as?"

"Right now, pulmonary hypertension is topping my list."

That stopped him in his tracks. Tanya's transplant had been due to primary pulmonary hypertension, but in a child? "You know that's a pretty uncommon finding in kids."

"Yes, and that's what has me worried."

He could imagine. Even though his specialty was transplantation, every time they could save a patient from needing one was a victory for the hospital and the patient, as well.

"Have you already set up another appointment with her?"

"No, I wanted to see what your schedule was like next week."

"That's funny, I was just about to call you to ask the same thing. I have next Wednesday off, if you're still interested in going to see what the Big Apple has to offer."

His suggestion was met with silence. Maybe she was checking her calendar. Or maybe she'd simply hung up on him. The latter didn't seem very likely. He hadn't done anything to make her mad. At least he didn't think so, not today. Then she came back on. "Yes, I can do Wednesday. What time?"

"I'll leave that up to you. I have the whole day off, so we can spend part of it sightseeing or all of it."

"And my patient?"

This time it was Snow who flipped through his appointments. "Can you do Friday, late morning?"

"I have a surgery first thing, but I should be done by about eleven. Can we make it right after lunch?"

He was tempted to ask her out to lunch, but he knew that was not a good idea. He wasn't even sure how smart it had been to offer to take her to see the sights on Wednesday. As he'd learned the hard way, there were consequences for every choice you made in life. His ex had suffered the consequences of his marriage proposal. The one that had ended in divorce. But he'd learned his lesson. From now on, he would make choices that only affected him.

"Yes, that will work. Say one o'clock?"

"One o'clock it is. And do you have a time preference for Wednesday?"

"How long do you think it'll take me to see everything?"

He chuckled. "In New York City? We measure sightseeing in terms of weeks, not hours."

"I guess I was thinking about just the biggest of the big. Like the Statue of Liberty or something like that."

"Okay, we'll put that on our list of things to see. That might be an all-day affair, in and of itself, though. Between that and Ellis Island, there's a lot to see."

"Sounds good." There was a pause. "And thanks for being willing to see my patient."

He smiled. "You were willing to see mine. I can't promise that same kind of breakthrough, however."

"Just a second set of eyes is all I need, Snow."

He liked it when she said his name, although he wasn't sure why. Everyone he knew shortened his name to Snow, since Snowden seemed stuffy, somehow.

"Well, you've got them. I'll see you Wednesday, then?"

"Yes, see you then."

They ended the call, and he set his phone on the desk, staring at it for a minute. He couldn't help but feel he was making a mistake by taking her around New York. He could always call Nicola and ask if she'd be willing to do it. But, like Kirsten said, Nicola and Kaleb had a baby at home and it didn't seem fair to pull her away from her family with the hours she was still putting in at work.

No, he'd do it. He'd just remind himself of his reasons and make sure his mind didn't wander outside of those preset parameters. As long as he did that, everything would be just fine.

Why had she worn a skirt on a sightseeing trip? Well, for one thing, it was cooler than pants on a hot day like today. And, two, because she pretty much lived her life in these same loose gauzy garments. She hiked up the white fabric to her knees yet again so it didn't drag on the ground when she stepped into Snow's low sports car, making sure she then tossed the fabric back over her knees once inside. Her low black espadrilles were super comfortable, too, and her sleeveless black top was loose and lightweight.

This was the first time she'd seen Snow out of his customary khaki pants and button-down shirt, and she had to say, he'd taken her breath away when he'd met her beside the car. Dressed in black jeans and a red polo shirt with his blond hair shoved off his forehead, he looked lean and fit, and far too gorgeous for comfort.

If she was smart, she would make up an excuse as to why she suddenly couldn't go. Like an emergency. It wouldn't exactly be a lie, because she was feeling a bit panicked about going.

She did her best to distract herself from stealing glances at him. At the way those long surgeon's fingers curled around the steering wheel, his thumb absently brushing across the leather surface. Because if she didn't, she was going to imagine that thumb stroking over her skin.

Yep, she might be in need of an emergency intervention. Had she learned nothing from her relationship with Dave? Yes, she had. That was part of the problem.

"So will the ferry stop at the Statue of Liberty first or Ellis Island?" It was pretty early in the morning, but Snow said if they left too late the line to get on the ferry at Battery Park would be very long.

He glanced her way, blue eyes surprisingly warm this morning. "The Statue of Liberty. I was able to get reservations to explore the platform, but the number of slots to climb to the crown are pretty limited. There wasn't enough lead time to try. And we'd have to climb the equivalent of twenty stories of steps to get to the top."

"Wow, that's a lot. I bet the view is amazing, though."

His thumb stopped stroking and his hands tightened slightly on the wheel. "Yes. The view is amazing even without the climb."

Had he taken someone special up there? Because his voice had had a funny timbre to it. Maybe he hadn't wanted to go up there with her. No, he'd said there were only a small number of people allowed up each day, which was understandable.

"I'll make it up there someday." She hoped, anyway. If her plans came to fruition, she might only be here for a couple of years before leaving for good. But no need to share that with him. Better *not* to tell him, actually. She hadn't even discussed it with her dad yet, although he would be thrilled if she came back home.

The problem was, her mom was buried in Ohio. Even though Kirsten knew her essence was not in those ashes, it would still be hard to leave the country, knowing she'd probably never be back to visit her grave.

A lump formed in her throat. As the only child, it would mean the grave would sit there all alone. Forever. Something far worse than eating alone at a restaurant.

She shook off a wave of melancholy. She was supposed to be here to enjoy the sights, not brood over things she couldn't control.

"Maybe you and Nicola can plan a day when her baby is older."

"Maybe." She forced her voice to be light and cheery. She was not going to spoil this day. Nothing like having him basically tell her this was their one and only outing. He'd as much as said he was doing it in appreciation for her help with Tanya. And because he hadn't been very friendly during their first interaction on the phone.

Why should his reasons matter? She barely knew him. And he didn't know her at all. It was already kind of him to have offered to take her in the first place. It's just that it made her feel like some friendless charity case.

Well, she wasn't a charity case, but she was still basically friendless at this point, although she was starting to form some connections that looked promising.

Like with Snow? No, not with him. Maybe it was better to hurry and get this over with. "How far away is the ferry station?"

"About a half-hour drive in this traffic. Not far. Once we get on the ferry, the trip will be pretty quick. About five minutes to the statue itself."

"Wow. Somehow I thought it was farther out than that."

"Nope. Not far at all. Ellis Island is pretty amazing, as well."

"I bet." She'd heard of the island, but honestly hadn't thought she'd get a chance to see it. At least not anytime soon. Her hours at the hospital had been pretty hectic ever since she'd arrived to take Dr. Billings's place.

"Did you get to see the sights when you were in Ohio?"

"Yes, but my mom was so sick at first…" She took a deep breath and tried again. "She didn't get to see much at all of America."

He glanced at her again as he stopped at a red light. "I'm sorry, Kirsten. That had to have been a hard time for your family."

"It was. I know how lucky I am to have had her with us for as long as we did, but it still wasn't an easy time. My dad really held our family together during that time."

"That's great. Not everyone has that kind of luxury."

What luxury? Of having a dad? She guessed not. "I didn't think of it as a luxury at the time. In fact, my dad and I butted heads a lot."

"Yeah. That I can understand. But he was a good father?"

What a strange question. A shiver went over her at the implications behind it. She'd been very lucky in that her family had been a loving and nurturing one. She guessed not everyone had that. But the way he'd asked it… "Yes. My dad is a wonderful man. We have a very close relationship. At least we do now."

He nodded, but didn't look her way. "I'm glad."

And if she'd said he wasn't a good father? She blinked as a thought flickered in her head and then disappeared. She decided maybe she'd better move the subject away from her own life. "So are your parents both still living?"

"Yes."

The word came out quickly, and she waited for him to add something. Anything. She'd been looking at him when she asked the question, and was shocked by the sudden change in his profile after he bit out his answer. A muscle bunched in his jaw, flickering just like that lost thought from a few seconds ago. After the silence grew past the point of discomfort, she realized he wasn't going to expand on his answer. Maybe his family wasn't as close as she and her parents had been. As she and her father still were.

She swallowed. Her question had been innocent, but she suddenly felt she'd stumbled into an area that boasted a huge No Trespassing sign. "Sorry, Snow. I didn't mean to pry. I was just—"

"No. Don't be sorry." His shoulders relaxed and one side of his mouth quirked. "I deserved it. I pried into your family history, didn't I?"

She hadn't minded, because she had nothing to hide. Unlike Snow, evidently. There was a sense that his one-word answer had been loaded with a meaning she didn't understand. And it had nothing to do with language or culture.

"I didn't consider it prying. Still. I shouldn't have asked."

"Yes, you should have. My parents are still alive, but my father and I have no contact. Nor will we. My mom lives in Massena, actually. It's considered part of upstate New York."

"Upstate?"

"It means in the northern part of the state."

"Ah, I see." She couldn't imagine being estranged from one of her parents. It would take something drastic and terrible to have made her turn away from either of them. That earlier thought flickered again, getting a little brighter this time.

That extra lock on his door…

Surely not. Maybe it wasn't Snow who was hiding something and needed to keep people from discovering it. Maybe it had something to do with his dad. Maybe Snow didn't want him getting in his office. Except she didn't keep medication of any kind in her office, and she was pretty sure it would be against hospital regulations, anyway.

And she was probably reading way too much into all of this.

Snow pulled into the parking lot of a coffee chain. "I need a cup of coffee. Do you want something?"

"That sounds good. Some cream and a couple of sugar packets to go in it, please."

After placing the order and sliding up to the window, he handed her coffee across. She took a bracing sip, glad for the slight burn that trickled down her throat. It was going to be a warm day, but it always surprised her that coffee tended to cool her down rather than make her even warmer.

Maybe it was the contrast of the beverage compared to the air inside the car.

Ten minutes later, they were pulling into the ferry station, and Snow found a place to park. There was already a line, but compared to what she'd been imagining, it wasn't too bad. They were just loading one of the ferries now.

"How many can it hold?"

"Several hundred passengers."

Her eyebrows went up as they got in line. "It shouldn't take us long to get on at that rate."

In actuality, they made it onto the ferry that was loading, although the line cut off a few people behind them. They went up the ramp to the boat and somehow managed to find a place near the railing, where they could see.

Then they were pulling away from the dock. A swift breeze blew into her face, and she was glad she'd scraped back her hair into a messy bun. It wouldn't have mattered if it had been neat, anyway, because most of it would probably be blown down by the time they got to the island.

Someone with a camera came over and

squeezed into the space next to her, forcing her to move over until her hip pushed against Snow's. "Sorry," she murmured.

He leaned down, a hint of aftershave tickling her nose. "Not your fault." His voice was low, rumbling against her ear in a way that made her shiver.

She swallowed as unfamiliar sensations skipped through her belly, setting fire to whatever composure she had left. What would it be like to have this man whisper to her in a darkened room?

Not something she was ever likely to experience. And if she wasn't careful these ludicrous ideas were going to taint all of her future interactions with him. Was she in danger of developing a little crush on the handsome doctor? She hoped not, because that wouldn't be smart, given how aloof he was most of the time. And how secretive. While she'd shared quite a bit of personal information with him, the second she'd asked him to share something in return, he'd pretty much cut her off. Kind of the way Dave had cut her off at the end of their relationship. He'd gone from being her lover to immersing himself in his studies to barely answering her texts. For Kirsten, who was used to an open and warm home environment, that kind of attitude was strange and unfamiliar. But maybe it was just the American way.

Except she had known lots of other Americans in the ten years she'd been in the States. And while there were always some outliers, she'd met some incredible people. Like Nicola and Kaleb.

None of that mattered, however. Because letting herself fantasize about a man she worked with, a man she was likely to never see again if she left for Lebanon, was not a very smart idea. Because she would end up doing what Dave had done to her: walk away.

But you can look, can't you, Kirsten? And if you're leaving...

She was pretty sure she was already guilty of looking. But actually, her leaving might make it even easier. Because there would be no long-term commitments. No painful goodbyes. And Snow was pretty obviously not a warm and fuzzy, "forever" kind of guy. Even Nicola had mentioned yesterday that Snow was divorced and hard to get to know.

She'd been surprised he was even taking her sightseeing.

So maybe Snow's attitude wasn't something she should take personally.

The person who'd squeezed next to her unexpectedly raised his arms to take a picture, and Kirsten jerked to the side, barely avoiding being elbowed in the chin. Snow must have noticed her evasive maneuver, because his arm went around her, and he edged her even closer. It wasn't with any kind of ulterior motive other than to help move her away from her annoying neighbor. It worked, and she found she could lean her head against Snow's shoulder. She rationalized it by telling herself it wasn't like she'd have to face him for the next twenty years. It might only be the next twenty months. Maybe less than that.

Then his thumb moved on her bare shoulder. Just like it had on his steering wheel. Just like she'd imagined him doing to her.

And boom! The thoughts she'd had while watching him drive hit all over again, skimming over her body and making her nipples tighten. Her knees went wobbly and she gripped the railing for support. Oh, Lord, she was going to have to learn to control herself. But unlike Snow, who seemed to be perfectly in control of his emotions and unaffected by her proximity, she wasn't used to having men pressed against her like this. Other than Dave, of course. She hadn't been in to casual dating, and he'd been her first real love. Her first time sleeping with a man.

She'd thought it would last forever, at the time. But evidently what she'd thought was a serious relationship hadn't been, at least not in his mind. They'd had some good times, but once they both left medical school and had started working in their prospective fields, it was like she'd been wiped off his slate of acquaintances. Added to that, their backgrounds were totally opposite.

His parents were divorced, and he had little contact with either of them, nor did he wish to change that. And he hadn't understood why she wanted to include her dad in every decision she made. It had caused a lot of friction between them. Maybe it was a matter of culture, but she didn't think so. They were just different. Too different. And to have it end after she'd bared her soul to him had devastated her, made her far less willing to share parts of herself with other people.

And yet she'd told Snow about her mom. About her reasons for going into pulmonology. She wasn't even sure why she had. But she wasn't doing it again.

She was not going to get any ideas about Snow. And even if by some weird chance she came to care about him, they would fare no better than she and Dave had. He wasn't close to his family, by his own admission. And he was definitely not a very warm person. Or someone who shared things from his innermost being.

Not that she would. Come to care about him, that was. Because it wouldn't last. Even if she decided not to move.

Right now, though, none of that mattered. She wasn't looking for permanent things. Not even in her job at NYC Memorial. So she could sit back and enjoy being pressed close to someone who was very attractive. And if what Nicola had said was true, that he was hard to get to know, that could work in her favor. Because she wouldn't need to try to get to know him. Leaning against him was temporary. In a few minutes, even that would be over and they would go back to being two strangers.

But for now, she intended to be present in the moment and enjoy this outing. She would ignore those tiny warning lights that were flashing far in the distance. There was still a lot of time to make a detour around them. A lot of time to avoid the emotional sinkhole that might lie just beyond.

At least she hoped there was.

CHAPTER FOUR

SNOW HADN'T BEEN able to help himself.

That jerk had almost clocked Kirsten with his elbow and hadn't even apologized. What he should have done, though, was switch places with her rather than put his arm around her. Because when she'd laid her head on his shoulder...

Every protective instinct he had had risen to the occasion. Along with something else that had nothing to do with protection. Snow normally controlled every emotion that came into existence, only allowing them out after he'd examined them for any sign of irregularity. And the ones he'd had just now? They'd rushed out before he was even aware of them. Impulsive. Unexpected. Taking him completely by surprise. And that scared the hell out of him. Because what if one of them wrested control from him?

But the choice now was to nudge her away from him, and how was that being any less of a jerk than the eager tourist on her other side? The truth was, despite that fear, he kind of liked the feeling of having a woman leaning against him again. The most he'd done since his divorce was pass the time with a couple of women he barely knew. And they'd been the ones who'd pursued him, not the other way around. Unfortunately, one of them had been a nurse from a different department at the hospital who had sent him a barrage of text messages afterward, asking if he was interested in dinner. In a movie. In more of the same. "Just as friends, of course." Well, he didn't believe that, so he'd finally met with her and had a very uncomfortable discussion. It had worked. She hadn't texted him again. Nicola told him later that she'd spread some pretty nasty rumors about him to anyone who would listen.

He did not want to wind up in another situation like that. So he'd decided the best course of action was to stay as aloof as possible. And not talk about his past, if he could help it.

The boat docked with a gentle bump, and the tourist leaned over the rail, still snapping shot after shot of the Statue of Liberty, before finally moving away.

Kirsten's head lifted from its perch, leaving him with a strangely empty feeling. He uncurled his arm, noticing her face was pink-tinged.

"I'm sorry about that."

He smiled. "Again, not your fault."

It wasn't his, either, so why was *he* feeling so guilty? Ever since the nurse incident, he'd worried about sending the wrong signals, even though he'd gone over and over the events leading up to them sleeping together. The nurse had sat at his table at a hospital fundraiser and had made eyes at him all night. She'd asked him to dance when the music had turned slow. One thing had led to another and he'd left with her, only to regret it almost immediately afterward. Especially when those messages started hitting his in-box.

He did not want a repeat of that situation.

Or the feeling of having no control over a situation.

Like this one? Maybe.

So why was he taking Kirsten on a sight-seeing trip?

Maybe because she seemed lonely somehow...and hinted that she might not be at NYC Memorial for the long haul. And because he truly was grateful for the help she'd given him with Tanya.

They stood and joined the line to disembark. Maybe it was time to turn things back toward work. "So why don't you tell me about your patient. The one you want me to look at on Friday."

A tiny frown marred her brow. "Oh, um, I didn't bring her file with me."

"I didn't expect you to. I'm just interested in knowing some more about the case." *And shaking myself back to reality.*

"Oh, okay."

So she described what had happened on each of the previous visits along with the treatments she'd tried. "I'm not convinced anymore that it's a recurrent bronchial infection. Even a viral cause would either get better or worse, not just hang there indefinitely with no response to medication."

"You've ruled out neoplasms?"

A neoplasm was an abnormal growth of cells. While some neoplasms were benign, they could still cause inflammation that acted as a trigger for other symptoms.

They walked down the gangway and then down the long pier that separated New York from New Jersey. "No. I'm hoping to do that on Friday with an MRI." She stepped onto Liberty Island itself and stared at the towering statue in front of them. "Oh, wow. That's amazing. And huge."

With its pedestal half the size of the monument itself, the Statue of Liberty was an impressive sight. "It's something, all right. I'm sorry we won't be able to go all the way to the crown."

"It's really okay. I'm just happy to be able to see it at all." She turned back toward him. "Sorry. We were in the middle of talking about my patient."

"We can do that later. You didn't come here to talk about hospital stuff."

He needed to remember that. Even though he'd decided he needed to keep things professional, he was forgetting that not all women were like his ex, whom he should have been able to trust with his deepest secrets, but had never been able to get beyond the edges of the truth. Or even like the nurse down in Maternity. And Kirsten had shown no signs of being interested in him. Even putting her head on his shoulder had probably been an attempt at staying out of reach of that tourist. She hadn't meant anything by it at all. He'd been the one to haul her closer, for God's sake.

They worked in overlapping medical fields, so it was natural that they would get to know each other a little more than if they worked in separate departments. He just needed to find the line that separated personal and professional and do his best not to stray onto the wrong side of it.

They walked the distance to the sculpture itself. "The Statue of Liberty was actually placed inside Fort Wood, which had points like a star. It makes a perfect base."

"It does. I can't get over how big it is. Much larger than I expected."

He tried to see it through her eyes, which

wasn't hard. Although he'd been here many times, its sheer size and presence still inspired awe. "It is big."

"So we get to go up into the…what did you call it?"

"The pedestal. And, yes, we have tickets. There are actually some interesting things housed in the building. We can either take the steps up to it or there's an elevator that goes most of the way."

"I think I need the exercise, if that's okay with you."

Perfect. He could use some time to regain his footing, anyway. "It's fine. I just wasn't sure with your…" He nodded at her skirt and shoes. She looked cool and comfortable, and far too beautiful.

And there he went again. Even more reason to take the slower route.

"It's kind of my go-to wear. And my shoes are almost as comfortable as tennis shoes. Now if my skirt was short, I might be going with the elevator, for obvious reasons."

Ha! Obvious reasons. Reasons he didn't need to be thinking about.

They wandered around the lower portion of the pedestal, and Snow pointed out different sights. "You'll see a lot more from the top of the building."

They trekked up the two hundred odd stairs that led to the center of the building. Snow frowned, then looked at his phone. "They used to have the old torch in here, I'm not sure... Ahh, they moved it to the new museum a couple of years ago. I should have looked to see. But this is what it looked like."

Kirsten came to stand next to him, looking at the image on his phone. "Oh, wow. Gorgeous. Why did they decide to replace it?"

"It was getting worn and the seals were leaking, letting water inside. After a while it wasn't feasible to keep trying to patch it up."

She glanced at him. "Sounds like what you do at the hospital. Replace things that can't be patched up."

"I never thought of it that way before." She had a point. "But the best course of action is to try to repair things so they don't need to be replaced."

She sighed. "It doesn't always work out that way, though, does it? Sometimes things just can't be repaired no matter how hard we try."

Like his childhood? His marriage? But in those particular situations, there were no transplants that would have allowed his dad to become a normal father, or that would have allowed Snow's marriage to live and thrive.

"You're right. Sometimes they can't be repaired."

She leaned back to look up at him. "I'm worried that my young patient might be one of those. I know children have transplants, too, but that's a lot of years to live with the immunosuppressant medications and the fear of eventual rejection. Or cancer."

"Yes, it is. But the alternative is death." That's exactly what had happened to his marriage. To his relationship with his dad.

"Yes. It is."

Was she thinking about her mom? He hadn't meant to put it quite so bluntly, but his thoughts had been chaotic over the last hour. "That came out a little harsher than it should have. And I'm sorry. Sometimes things just don't move quickly enough to save people."

She studied his face, her brow clearing. "You're talking about my mom."

"Yes."

"She just couldn't hold on until an organ became available, and at the end, she went on hospice care so they could keep her comfortable. It was no one's fault. It's kind of a crapshoot at times, isn't it? The whole transplant process."

"Yes, it's a matter of luck and timing."

Luck. Both good and bad. Good for the recipient, but terrible for the ones having to make heartbreaking decisions about loved ones.

Maybe she sensed his thoughts because she touched his hand. "I don't envy you your job, Snow. You're the patient's last stop. Their last hope. Most of the time, I'm not. If I run out of options, and they're still young and healthy enough, I can refer their cases to you and wash my hands of them."

Somehow, he doubted she washed her hands of them. Even when the patient wasn't hers, like Tanya.

"Except not everyone is eligible for a transplant." He turned over his hand and curled his fingers around hers. "And that is the hardest thing of all. Deciding who has the best odds for a successful outcome."

"Yes, it is. I remember the moment a doctor told my mom she was terminal. He wasn't very kind about it, just kind of chilly and detached, like he'd already handed her over to death. I vowed I would never be that kind of doctor. Except it's not that easy. If you allow yourself to feel everyone's pain…" Something shimmered in her blue eyes. "Well, I wouldn't be able to help the next patient or the one after that, if I couldn't get past my emotions. But it's hard. Really hard. There are just some patients…"

Like the one she wanted him to look at? For Snow, who was so used to controlling his feelings, he probably came across like the doctor who had told Kirsten's mother she was terminal. It wasn't intentional. And he wasn't trying to be cruel—or detached, like she'd said—but there was an element of self-preservation involved. Like there'd been during his childhood, when survival mode was the only mode under which he knew how to operate. Bits and pieces of that instinct still came out at times, and although he no longer feared for his life, deciding which emotions to pull out of hibernation was not an easy thing. He'd learned that during his marriage.

Sometimes it had been damn near impossible. Especially since there were times he still woke up in a cold sweat, thinking he heard something rattling his doorknob. He still locked his bedroom door at night to try to ward off those dreams.

Damn! Not something he needed to think about right now.

"Yes, you're right. It is hard." He released her hand, curling his fingers into his palms instead. "But being a doctor was never about being easy."

"No, I suppose not. But there are times when I relish the easy cases. The ones that I can solve and they stay solved. Those have happy endings."

"I think we all relish those types of cases."

She pulled her gaze toward one of the windows, seeming to shake away her thoughts. "So what are the views like up here?"

"They're great. Ready to see?"

"Yes. I'm definitely ready."

The sun was sinking low in the sky by the time they got through the Liberty Museum and visited Ellis Island. Back on the ferry once again, she realized she was exhausted, and despite her reassurances that her shoes were comfortable, her feet were a little more tired than they should have been. She slid her feet partly out of them and curled her toes before putting the shoes halfway on again.

"Hurting?"

"Yes, a little bit. I think they would have been tired even in tennis shoes, though. Sandals would have been worse."

"Probably. Especially on those stairs."

"Ah, yes, the stairs. Was I the one who actually suggested we go up them, rather than use the elevator?"

He grinned. "You were. Regretting it now?"

"Not exactly regretting, but wishing I was about twenty years younger."

His smile turned into a laugh. "You're not exactly ancient, Kirsten. You're what? Thirty? Thirty-one?"

"Thirty-two."

"Oh…so you *are* ancient."

She jabbed his arm. "That's not very nice." She knew he was joking, but it was more fun to pretend offense.

"No one has ever accused me of being nice."

Was he serious? Maybe. Hadn't she thought he matched his name, when she first met him? But she was finding that he had his moments. Like when he'd pulled her closer to help distance her from that tourist who was busy taking photos. "You're not so bad. Most of the time." She smiled to take away the sting. "Thanks for today, by the way. I had fun. I had no idea there was so much to see on the islands. At this rate, though, it will take me years to see all of New York."

"You have plenty of time."

She didn't. Not really. But she wasn't going to tell him that. And she was not going to ask him to go with her again. Once was enough. Why? Because she'd enjoyed today a little too much. "I'll start making my list of things to see."

"Well, at least you can check one item off of it."

"It's going to be hard to outdo what I saw today." She forced her feet back into her shoes as she spied the dock up ahead. In a few moments they would be getting off the boat and heading back to their normal everyday routines. She had to admit, there was a small part of her that didn't want today to end. And that wasn't good. Because everything came to an end, eventually. Everything.

The boat docked and everyone stood. The second she put weight on her aching feet, they protested and she realized the right one had gone to sleep from the way she'd been sitting. Her foot felt nothing. But she knew well enough that pins and needles would soon erupt beneath her sole, making her want to laugh and cry all at the same time. Yikes.

Snow, who'd been waiting for her to move forward, tilted his head. "Are you okay?"

"My foot's asleep."

As the crowd surged toward the exit, she realized she was in danger of getting caught up in the moving stream. Snow put an arm around her waist. "Hold on to me."

Just in time, because they were going whether they were ready or not. She snaked her arm around his lean hips and forced herself to move, leaning most of her weight on him and hoping her foot was landing flat.

"Sorry. It has to be the way I was sitting. It'll wake up in a minute."

And it did. Seconds later, those familiar waves of prickles came every time she took a step. She groaned aloud in frustration.

He smiled down at her. "I take it it's waking up."

"Ugh. How can you tell?"

They somehow made it off the boat and Snow led her to a nearby bench. "Sit down for a second."

She did as he asked. "Thanks. Kind of embarrassing that I didn't notice it while I was sitting."

"It happens."

The sun was starting to go down and as Kirsten looked at the skyline, which had streaks of red appearing over the tops of the buildings, her foot was soon forgotten. "It's so beautiful. Sometimes life gets so busy, I forget to enjoy moments like these."

"Yes. Me, too."

Something in his voice urged her to look at him. And when she did, there was an emotion in his face that looked familiar. And terrifying.

Those light blue eyes were on her and not

on the sky. And in those eyes she thought she saw...

Longing. Desire. Myriad things she'd been pretty sure she'd never see again before she left the country. And things she was positively sure she'd never see in Snow's face. Was he even capable of feeling those things?

Evidently, because there it was. And he wasn't trying to look away or brush it off as something else entirely. No. He didn't care that she'd noticed. Or recognized it for what it was.

Or maybe that was all in her imagination.

"Give me your foot." He reached his hand down.

Without hesitation, she lifted her leg and let him haul it onto his lap. His nimble fingers tipped off her shoe and set it on the bench next to his hip as her mouth went dry.

Was he going to—?

He palmed her bare arch, kneading the spots where her nerve endings had gone haywire. Except they weren't anymore. But something stopped her from admitting that fact or telling him that he didn't need to massage it. Because it felt wonderful. Heavenly, even.

She couldn't suppress the soft groan that slid out before she could stop it.

"Good?"

"Mmm…yes. I didn't realize how tired they were." She gave a nervous laugh when he shifted his touch to the base of her toes. "I'm not going to want to get up, if you keep that up."

He smiled. "No need to get up just yet. Neither of us are working tonight, so we don't have to go directly home, unless you're tired."

His thumbs were nudging pressure points on the sole of her foot, bewitching her and removing any desire to get up and get moving.

It was luscious. Her ex had never been a touchy-feely person, so there'd been no back massages, no little unexpected touches. Most of their physical connection happened in the bedroom. And for this to occur out in the open… She felt a little bit like an exhibitionist as she leaned her head on the back of the hard bench and gave herself over to his ministrations. Right now she didn't care who saw. And it wasn't like they were making out. Or anything else.

"Aren't your feet tired at all?"

"No." The one-word answer surprised her enough that she almost pulled away. Except he was now working on the base of her toes, moving the joints this way and that. It wasn't hurting anything to enjoy his touch. Like she'd thought earlier, she was not here in New York on a permanent basis. So she needed to soak up what she could while she was here. And if that meant a little bit of physical contact between her and the transplant surgeon, so be it. After all, she was a transplant herself. One that would soon be uprooted and planted somewhere else in a short period of time.

Why not just give in to what had been building for most of the day? She'd be lying to herself to say she wasn't attracted to him. She'd already reacted to his nearness. More than once.

But what about him? The difference between right now and her very first conversation with him was worlds apart. And she was pretty sure he'd been aware of her while they were talking about repairs and transplants.

She swallowed. Only one way to know for sure.

"Snow…" She whispered his name, half-hoping he wouldn't hear her. But he did. And when his eyes met hers, she saw that she hadn't been wrong. There was a heat burning in those pupils that surprised her. Ignited her.

His massaging fingers slowed, until they were no longer moving. Everything in their little bubble of space grew still as they stared at each other.

Then he finally lifted her foot from his lap and set it on the ground. She gulped, thinking she'd read him wrong, that he was going to get up and suggest they go back to the car. Then his arm snaked around her waist, just like it had on the boat. When he'd been trying to protect her. Only this time it was not protection she saw on his face.

This moment seemed inevitable, felt like they'd been hurtling toward it ever since they'd stepped foot on that boat.

And Kirsten couldn't stop it if she wanted to. And, Lord help her, she didn't want to.

When his fingers threaded in the hair at her nape and he tilted her face up, she was lost in a sea of blue. Her teeth came down on her lip, and his eyes flicked to her mouth. And then his head was descending in slow motion, and her world suddenly tilted on its axis.

CHAPTER FIVE

HE HADN'T MEANT to kiss her, had only meant to help with her foot. But then she'd said his name. The husky way it rolled off her tongue had made him come unglued, had pulled him toward her. And hell if her mouth wasn't every bit as soft as he'd imagined it would be. Her skin held a hint of salt from the spray of the boat trip. In trying to help her foot wake up, he woken himself, instead.

Pull away. Before it's too late. Before you're out of control.

The warning was already too late, because the second she started kissing him back, he was free-falling. Adrift in the sky with nothing tethering him to reality.

And right now, reality was the last thing he wanted to think about.

He bit her lower lip, and she shuddered

against him, her arms looping themselves around his neck. He needed to take a step back, to make a decision. Get up and force himself to take her home. Or get up and take her back to his apartment to finish what he started. Because staying on this bench wasn't an option, unless he wanted to get them thrown in jail. Or maybe he should let her make the decision and take the choice out of his hands.

He leaned down and found her ear. "How anxious are you to get home?"

"Not anxious. Especially if I'll be there alone."

A wave of exhilaration crashed over him. It hadn't been his imagination. She was just as caught up in the moment—in him—as he was in her.

"You won't be alone, I promise. And I was thinking my place."

Her cheek slid against his, her arms tightening and holding her against him. "Your place it is."

"Can you walk?"

She leaned back and glanced into his face. "It's a little too early to be asking me that, isn't it?"

He laughed, catching her drift. "I was referring to your foot. But I've always liked a challenge."

Her face turned a wonderful shade of pink. "I wasn't suggesting... I thought you meant..."

"Oh, I know what you thought." He grinned. "So...your foot? Or would you rather I carry you back to the car."

"I can walk on it."

"Too bad. I was kind of looking forward to tossing you over my shoulder."

"You wouldn't!"

The way he was feeling right now, he wasn't too sure what he would do. But nothing about this felt ominous or truly dangerous to anything other than his own peace of mind.

Snow aimed a slow smile at her before taking her shoe and sliding it back in place. "Okay. No shoulders. At least not today." Then, taking her hand, he towed her toward the parking lot and his car. He hadn't set out on this trip with this endgame in mind. In fact, he'd tried to avoid this with every fiber of his being. But now that it was here, and she was just as into it as he was, he wasn't going to shy away from it. Even if he wanted to. And he definitely did *not* want to.

What about future text messages?

He wasn't sure how he knew it, but Kirsten wouldn't go that route. She hadn't been the one to initiate this—he had. And that should bother him on some level.

They made it to the car and headed out of the parking lot. He caught her hand in his and placed it on the gearshift. The sensuality of their hands together as they shifted from one gear to another made desire clutch at his innards. They stopped at a traffic light, and Snow pulled her toward him for a long, drawn-out kiss. A half hour had never seemed so long.

Then they were back in traffic. New York City definitely had a nightlife, so the line of vehicles was almost as long as it was during rush hour. He could see why some people chose not to have a vehicle, relying instead on public transport to get them where they needed to be. Kirsten had said that was part of the appeal of the city. Snow liked to drive himself, though, despite the inconveniences.

"Just a few more minutes, I promise."

She gave him a smile. "Don't worry. I'm enjoying the ride."

Something about the way she said that made his insides heat. Then again, it could just be him reading a secondary meaning into her words. He was tempted to find an empty lot and find out, but he really, really wanted to do this in his apartment, rather than in public. He wanted privacy. And leg room. And to enjoy her in small, sensuous bites. He could dissect all the feelings that went along with that desire later. But most of all, he wanted her naked, with her skin against his. Anything less than that would be…sacrilege.

A few blocks later, his apartment complex came into view. He pulled down a ramp, punched in his code and waited as the doors swung open. He'd rented this place six years ago, before he married Theresa. And after she left, he'd retained the apartment, although he'd thought about selling when they first divorced. But since not all of his memories in this place were linked to her, he was able to get past it. Besides, he already had his security measures in place, and to get something else… Well, it meant he had to make a decision about whether or not to cycle back through the measures he'd taken ever since he'd been out on his own. By keeping this place, he didn't have to make that decision. Could just pretend that it was easier to leave things as they were, than to have to deal with putting his past behind him, once and for all.

If he sat down and examined it long enough, he'd realize that no, he probably wouldn't have his extra locks removed. And that idiosyncrasy had played a part in the breakup of his marriage. A smaller part than the issues she'd had with his emotional availability, to be sure, but it all had jumbled together to make a huge mess of their relationship.

There'd been no saving it by that point. And maybe there'd been no saving him, by that point, either.

He found his parking place and pulled into it, shifting his car into first gear and turning off the engine. Kirsten had gotten quiet. A little too quiet. Maybe she'd changed her mind.

Hell, if she had, it was better to find out now than later. "Hey. Are you okay?"

"Not really."

His chest tightened, and he somehow forced the words from a throat that had gone dry. "Do you want me to take you home?"

"What?" Understanding dawned in her face. "No. I didn't mean that. I meant I didn't expect the trip over here to take as long as it did."

His muscles went slack with relief, and he laughed, swinging out of his car and moving around to open her door. "I'm afraid it's going to take a whole lot longer."

"What do you mean?"

He took her hands and looked into her face. "If you think we're going in there and moving through everything at lightning speed, you're very much mistaken."

She used his grip to tug him toward her. "I don't care what speed we move at. As long as we move." She nodded at the corner of the parking garage, where a small camera silently watched. "Because that thing is going to get a…how do you say it…? *Hadhar*... To see more than it wishes to see."

He loved hearing her say things in Arabic. "I think *eyeful* is the word you're looking for. And you're right. It—or whoever is behind the scenes—is going to get an eyeful if we don't start walking toward the elevator."

Pressing his forehead to hers, he said, "There's a camera in the elevator, too, unfortunately."

"And in your apartment? Are there cameras there, too?"

She meant the words in a playful way, but his gut tightened for a second. Because there were. Only his cameras were very well hidden and could be turned off with the touch of a button. He was careful with how he phrased his answer. "No spying eyes in there. The only one watching you will be me. The only recording device will be in my head."

"I like that. So you'll be reliving it?"

"Will you?" He already knew his answer, but he wanted to know hers.

"You know I will."

He led her toward the elevator and pushed the button. Once inside, he used a special key that would take him to his assigned floor. Every tenant had one. It had been one of the features that had sold him on the place.

They arrived on the fourteenth floor, and

got off the elevator. Snow curled his fingers around her hips and walked backward with her toward the door to his apartment. Once there, he unlocked the dead bolt and the doorknob, and pressed his thumb on the reader pad, then waited for that last security measure to release a lock. As they started through the entryway, he saw her eyes were no longer on him, but on the door they'd just come through.

"I didn't realize these big apartment blocks had so much security," she said.

"It varies from place to place." She didn't need to know that only his apartment had all of these measures. She was only here for a night. Not long-term, like Theresa had been. No need to explain anything. Or try. Not that his ex had bought any of his explanations.

"Got it." But there had been a tiny hesitation before she'd said that.

Time to get her mind back on other things. He slammed the door and reeled her toward him. "Still okay?"

"Oh, yes." She smiled, and whatever he'd seen in her eyes disappeared in a flash. "And now that we're alone…"

"All alone. Not even a pet fish to interrupt us."

"Mmm… I like that. Not the pet thing, but the no-interruptions thing."

His hands went to her shoulders and skimmed down her arms. Her blouse had no sleeves and the skin he encountered was warm and silky soft. She was addicting, in the best possible way.

He reached down and scooped her up, heading toward his bedroom.

Laughing, she said, "What about the tour?"

"Don't worry. You're about to get the most important tour of the house. There's a lot to see." He kissed her cheek, her nose, her mouth. "And even more to explore."

His bedroom door was open, so he walked in, then turned to push it shut with his foot. She stopped him.

"No cameras, right? So no need to shut the door."

He blinked. "Right. Just habit."

It was habit. One ingrained since childhood, when his mom had whispered for him to get into his room and lock the door. Leaving a door wide-open was hard. Even now.

But he smiled and left it as it was, moving with her toward the bed. He set her on it carefully, smiling as she held her arms out to him.

He could shut the door later. It would be okay. It was actually the first time a woman had challenged him about his habit. Except for his ex. But even then, Theresa hadn't known the full reason behind it. She'd banged and banged at that door inside of his head, trying to get inside...to understand why he was the way he was. That had proved a disaster. Because the harder she pushed, the more he barricaded himself in. He wouldn't let a woman get close enough to try again.

And there was no need. Snow would honor the toast he and Kaleb had made a year ago—he was not getting married again. His buddy might have found his so-called soul mate, but he was pretty sure there wasn't one out there for him. And for his own peace of mind, he didn't want there to be.

Looking at the woman now sprawled across his bed, her eyes staring up at him as if waiting for his next move, all thoughts of Theresa—and the doors in his mind—fled as a wave of need coursed through him. The long white skirt emphasized her tanned skin and long slender legs. His glance went lower. "Let's get rid of these shoes, shall we?"

He leaned down and slid the black wedged heels off her feet. There was a small blister on the outside of one of her big toes. He touched it. "Damn. Why didn't you tell me about this?"

She looked puzzled. "Tell you what?"

"That your shoes were giving you a blister."

"I didn't really notice it until the very end."

That didn't help. He felt like a cad for making her walk as much as they had. He sat on the bed and propped her foot across his legs. "We can put some lotion on that."

She straightened her leg, forcing it off his lap. "Later. The last thing I want to talk about is blisters or shoes or lotion."

He shifted at the waist, using his arms to lean down and bracket her into his space. "So, what do you want to talk about instead?"

"Don't want to talk at all," she muttered, taking hold of his polo shirt and pulling him down toward her. The kiss was hard and wet and full of so much promise that it made his throat tighten. Oh, to be able to just live in this moment for a lifetime.

Well, the lifetime part might not be possible, but living in the moment was definitely doable.

The kiss deepened, until it was teeth and tongue and the need to get closer to each other. When he pulled away, his breath was uneven, the area behind his zipper throbbing with need. And her face. Kirsten's face was flushed, and her lips had parted to reveal the edges of white teeth.

"Damn. How did you do that?"

"Do what?"

"Push me to the very edge of the world." He stood to his feet and took hold of her skirt. "Is there a zipper?"

"No, it's elastic."

He tugged, and like magic it rode the curve of her hips, and he waited until she lifted slightly before tugging it over her butt. White lace came into view. Lace that was wide across her hips and narrowed to play peekaboo with the area at the junction of her thighs. He wanted to pause there. But he needed to finish his task. The skirt.

After letting it drop to the floor, his fingers trailed up the outsides of her thighs, enjoying more of her silky smooth skin. But first, the blouse had to go.

The buttons were black, like the rest of the fabric, and he leaned over her, going by feel rather than by sight as each pearl fastener slid through its hole and displayed more curves hidden beneath it. This time the lace was black, matching the fabric of her shirt. He liked it. Liked that her bra was the opposite color of her underwear. It reminded him of the turmoil and contradictions he housed inside himself.

"You're beautiful, did you know that?"

She smiled up at him, her eyes bright, shining just for him. At least right now. "You're not so bad yourself." She sat up, her fingers going to his waistband. "But I think it's time to even up the playing field."

Pushing his shirt up his stomach, he leaned over so she could haul the garment over his head. Then it was on the floor, her fingers wandering over his bare chest, scraping down over his nipples in a way that made

his breath whoosh out on an oath. He somehow managed to choke out, "That is not lev-
eling the field."

Using his legs to push hers apart, he joined
her on the bed, his erection pressing into her
belly with a need that was hard to contain.
He kissed her as one hand skimmed up her
side until he found her breast. It was soft,
her bra presenting it to him in a way that
made his mouth water. He did what she'd
done to him a moment or two ago, and gently
scraped his thumbnail over her nipple. Her
moan shot through him, arcing right down
to his shaft and making it jump.

Hell, with the way his emotions were cas-
cading out of control, he was not going to be
able to make this last as long as he'd hoped.
The horizon was moving toward him at an
ever-increasing speed. Soon he wouldn't be
able to stop it from slamming into him and
dragging him to a swift release.

Something about that niggled at the back
of his mind, a blinking red light that warned
him to slow down. But he didn't want to listen to it or anything, right now.

He reached behind her and unhooked her
bra, peeling it down her arms and tossing

it in the direction her blouse and shirt had gone. Then she was bare, that golden skin calling to him. He rolled over, pulling her with him, until she was straddling his hips, sitting up where he could see her, his gaze moving down her throat, over those beautiful breasts, past her stomach to the place where her legs parted for him.

Hard and throbbing and still struggling for control, he reached back to his pocket and removed his wallet. Took out a condom and threw the wallet onto his nightstand, missing and sending it sailing onto the floor. He didn't care. Nothing mattered right now except for getting the rest of their clothes off.

But he didn't want her to move.

He gripped her hips and rotated his pelvis into her.

Hell! Raw sensation rocketed through him, his mind teeming with tantalizing scenarios all ending with them finishing this right now, with their clothes still on. He repeated the act, letting himself fall a little further. Kirsten's eyes shut tight.

"No." Her word came out raspy and urgent.

He immediately sat up, that niggling at

the back of his mind becoming a screaming, accusing siren.

"I'm sorry." His arms going around her to keep her from falling backward. "Did I hurt you?"

She got off of him and stood on the hardwood floor. "No. You didn't." Before he could figure out why she suddenly wanted to stop, her fingers went to her waistband and pushed her panties down.

"I thought you said—"

"I meant 'no' as in I want to feel you, and if you keep doing what you're doing—" she gave a visible swallow "—I'm not going to last very long."

Her meaning hit him, and the relief was so thick, he had to shut his eyes for a minute to get through it. Then he laughed, although it was shaky. "Damn. I was just thinking that maybe we could make it work without taking our clothes off at all."

"You thought wrong." She reached for the button on his jeans and undid it.

In a flash he was off the bed and shucking the rest of his clothes. He grabbed the condom package and opened it, rolling it over himself. "Okay, so no to the clothes. But yes to everything else?"

"Yes, to everything…and anything."

The words blazed over him, setting him on fire and storming his senses. To have that kind of trust, even though she knew almost nothing about him…

His throat clogged for a second. He would make sure that trust wasn't misplaced. Would make sure of her pleasure, even if it meant withholding his own.

He took her wrists and pulled them behind her, until they rested in the small of her back. Holding them there, he leaned down and kissed her, some weird feeling sliding up his spine and burrowing in the back of his head.

God, he wanted to do everything. Thoughts came in snatches that he struggled to catch hold of. "I want you on top. I want your hands like this."

"Okay." The word was breathless. Excited.

He sat on the bed, still holding her hands behind her, and she scrambled on top of him, until she was straddling him once again. He wanted to watch her. Wanted to see each movement of her hips, each expression that crossed that beautiful face of hers. Slowly he reclined on the mattress.

"Lift your hips, honey." He wasn't exactly sure how this was going to work, but hell if he didn't want to try.

She raised up enough to free him. Then, looking at him, she found him, shifted until she was positioned over him. Then she sank onto him in tiny increments, slowly enveloping him in a way he'd never felt before. There was a sensuality to her that came naturally. There was nothing artificial, nothing scripted. His fingers entwined with hers, staying right there with her as she started to move. He should touch her, make sure she came to completion first, but there was something in her face. Something that said she didn't need anything extra.

So instead of letting go of her hands, he used his hold to tip her forward until he could reach her breasts, letting his lips and tongue glide over her, hold her, suckle her.

Her breath came faster, and every once in a while a soft sound escaped, driving him wild. He'd needed this night. Needed to find a release he hadn't found in a very long time.

He released her nipple and lifted his head

up so he could capture her mouth as she rose and fell faster, her movements becoming jerky and uncoordinated. God. He wanted to be right there with her. He plunged his tongue into her mouth, mimicking what she was doing above him. Suddenly she pulled away from him and sat up, her hips pumping, pelvis rotating each time it met his body.

Hell, she was pleasuring herself. "Oh, sweetheart. Damn, you are killing me."

Her face was intent, eyes tightly closed as she continued her movements. It was too much. He was going to...

She cried out, hips suddenly pumping hard, and he felt it. The pulsating squeeze and release on his shaft. He erupted, driving into her with a groan, mind blanking out for a few seconds, all thoughts obliterated as he hung in space, lost in his own incredible pleasure.

Kirsten relaxed against him for a few seconds, before rolling forward to lie half across his body, breathing hard. He let go of her hands and wrapped his arms around her, holding her close.

He'd meant to bring her here, have sex with her and then drive her home. But that wasn't enough. Not right now. Maybe it was the stupor of his climax. Maybe it was the unbridled sex itself. But he wanted more. Wanted her again. As dangerous or stupid as that might be.

So he held her as his mind finally began to unravel, a delicious lethargy beginning to steal over him as he relaxed completely. He didn't ask her to stay, although the impulse was there, knocking on the door of his mind. He'd let her decide. He waited. Struggling to overcome the heaviness in his limbs, the satiation that was spreading through every cell of his body, until he finally gave in to it.

With one last tightening of his arms, he let his eyes close so the darkness could overtake him.

CHAPTER SIX

KIRSTEN ROLLED OUT of bed and gathered her clothes. Wow. Okay, so the not-being-able-to-walk thing was real, but it was more because her legs were so shaky that she could barely make them hold her up. A squeaked laugh came out of her.

He was leaning against the headboard watching her, hands behind his head. He looked totally relaxed. Totally at ease. And totally capable of walking unaided.

The thought of him sauntering naked to the bathroom made her mouth go dry.

"What?" he said.

There was no way she was going to tell him, so she just shook her head. "I didn't expect to spend the night last night."

"I'm glad you did."

That surprised her. She hadn't really

thought the man housed any softer emotions. Even last night, he'd been all hard-edged and intense. And, actually, she was glad she stayed, too. Glad to see this transformation in him. She'd learned some things about him in the process. Her thoughts yesterday about how Snow and her ex were similar seemed completely off base now. They were nothing alike. Besides, she didn't need to worry about her heart being broken this time, because it hadn't been involved in what had happened last night.

And the sex had been...

Out of this world.

He'd woken and reached for her twice during the night and both times had topped the time before, which left her discombobulated, both mentally and physically.

Hence her uncooperative limbs. "I'm just going to jump in the shower, if that's okay."

One eyebrow went up. "Want some company?"

Her weak limbs somehow found new strength. She gave an internal eye roll. "As tempting as that sounds, I'll never make it to work on time if that happens." She reached for the doorknob and tried to twist it, but it didn't budge. She tried again, thinking it was just because she was shaky, but it still didn't move. A chill went over her. Hadn't she asked him to leave the door open last night?

"Why is this locked?"

His eyes went from warm and satisfied to cool and wary in the space of two seconds. He levered himself out of bed and came over to unlock the mechanism. And somehow not even his nakedness took the edge off her shock.

"Sorry," he said. "Force of habit."

Force of habit? Locking himself in his bedroom, when the rest of his apartment was already shut up tighter than a penitentiary?

She swallowed. Something about that didn't feel right. She'd told them he could do anything to her. And he had, but there'd been nothing sinister about any of it.

But the locked door…

She'd reminded him that they were alone. And yet, despite that, sometime during the night, he'd gotten up and not only *shut* the door, but also *locked* it.

The chill spread to her bones. Anything

personal she'd asked him had been met with short answers that told her nothing.

"Is there something I need to know?" First his office, and now his home.

He didn't meet her eyes this time. "Nope."

Another one-word answer, like when she'd asked about his parents. His later explanation hadn't been much more revealing. It was like he was withholding something. Something important.

He locked his bedroom door, even though he lived alone. Exactly whom was he expecting to try to get in?

Before she could stop herself a question came out. "Is someone *after* you, Snow?"

Maybe a disgruntled relative from a surgery gone bad? She'd certainly heard of that happening. And it would explain everything. Or almost everything.

The sudden pivot to face her came out of nowhere, causing her to take a step back. "What do you mean?" The wariness in his face had turned glacial, his jaw stiff, lips white. He might as well have been flash frozen.

Her idea didn't seem so ridiculous now. "I don't know. I've just never met anyone who lived alone and locked almost every door they had. I certainly don't do that. It just struck me as...odd."

Odd was the most neutral word she could think of. Because the other ones that were running through her head were things she wasn't going to give voice to.

"No one is after me."

He'd sidestepped her statement by answering her earlier question. So much for him not being like Dave. He'd evaded every question she threw at him as he was breaking up with her. She still had no idea what had gone wrong with that relationship. Had she been too clingy? Too ambitious? Was she horrible in bed? She had no idea, because he *wouldn't communicate with her*!

Well, fine. If Snow wanted to act like that, she had no horse in this race. But, something was going on. If he'd told her that New York could be a dangerous place to live, she would have accepted it at face value...but it took a special key to even get up to his apartment. And no one else at the hospital seemed to need an extra lock on their office door like he did. The hospital had pretty tight security. And cameras.

She made a decision. "Well, that's good to know. I think I'll skip the shower. Do you mind driving me home? I can catch a taxi, if not."

"Of course, I'll drive you." If anything, he looked relieved that she wasn't staying. Wasn't asking any more questions that he wasn't willing to answer. So much for his being glad that she'd stayed over.

Her perfect night had just imploded, and she wasn't even sure why. All she knew was that she needed to get home and clear her head before going to work. She definitely couldn't do that here. Not when her feelings for him had gone from simple lust to... She wasn't sure what these new emotions rolling around inside of her were. But she didn't like them. They spoiled everything she and Snow had done last night.

The sooner they could go back to being colleagues who worked together and nothing more, the better. All she needed to do now was figure out how to get there.

And how to forget the iciness of his demeanor when she'd asked about that lock on his door.

* * *

The look on Kirsten's face was going to haunt him for a long time. The shock when she'd turned the knob and realized she couldn't get out of his room had shifted to a flash of fear before the emotion disappeared. He remembered feeling that exact same thing as a kid, when his dad had rattled the doorknob to his room. The thought of doing something that made her afraid...

She'd asked why it was locked, and all he could think of to say was that it was out of habit.

It was.

But there were reasons behind the habit. Reasons he didn't want to explain, since she wasn't going to be in his life forever. And so the alternative was to clam up. She probably thought he was some kind of serial killer or something. She hadn't been able to get out of there fast enough.

All because of something he'd done.

Goddamn. This was why he didn't do relationships. Would never do them again. His past was his past, and not something he wanted to relive with every question. And he certainly didn't want someone to be afraid of him.

He'd tried sharing something with Theresa once, but the questions had kept coming in a never-ending barrage that had ended in cheating and divorce.

It was easier just to move through life without worrying about what others thought—when he himself didn't have to think about it. It was what it was, and he had no desire to change. For anyone.

Especially after what had happened with Kirsten.

Honestly? He should probably sit down and talk to her so that there was no weirdness between them.

No weirdness? How about sleeping together when they barely knew each other? How was that for weirdness? How about locking the door and scaring the crap out of her?

There was nothing normal about that.

Anger rose up in him in a wave. So what if he locked the damn door? He'd slept with two other women—women he didn't know very well—and it hadn't seemed to bother them. One had practically turned into a stalker afterward. So why was he suddenly so worried about what Kirsten thought?

Something inside of him, though, said that this time he needed to talk to her. To at least explain a little bit of what had happened to him. Before she got some crazy thoughts that weren't based in reality.

It boiled down to the fact that he didn't want her to be afraid of him. To think that he housed some kind of monstrous compulsion.

How can you be sure you don't?

His locked doors were a compulsion. He'd been able to admit that to himself a long time ago. But it didn't harm anyone. Or so he'd thought. Until this morning, when he'd looked into Kirsten's eyes and saw the size of her pupils.

Yes. He was going to pull her aside and talk to her. Maybe after they looked at her patient tomorrow. If she still wanted his opinion, that is. Maybe she wanted nothing to do with him now.

No, he had a feeling that Kirsten's patients came first with her, no matter how uncomfortable things might get with her personal life.

That could work in his favor, if he was careful.

A knock came at his office door, and he tensed. If it was Kirsten, he hadn't quite made a decision about how much to tell her.

"Come in."

It wasn't the pulmonologist who came through the door, though—it was Kaleb. Relief poured through him. He forced a smile. "Hey! I've haven't seen you around in a couple of weeks. How are Nicola and the baby?"

His friend came in and dropped into one of the chairs in front of his desk. "They're doing fine. I'm finally back at work after taking a week off to stay home and watch the baby while she recovered from RSV."

"I didn't realize she had that. No problems?"

Kaleb leaned back. "No, just fussiness and a lack of sleep. For both of us."

"You, fussy?"

"Ha! Funny. You try taking care of a sick baby and see how well you do."

"I can't see myself doing that. Ever." He changed the subject before Kaleb read more into the words than he should. "I saw Nicola around the hospital a couple of times, but just from a distance. She looked busy."

"Yeah, her schedule was more hectic than mine last week, which is why I was the one to stay with Cass."

"No lasting problems from the RSV?"

Kaleb adored his baby and Nicola. It was there in his eyes every time he talked about either of them. And Snow was glad for him. The pact they'd made may not have worked out for the facial reconstructive surgeon. In fact, it had seemed to backfire royally, as Nicola got pregnant after a one-night stand. But the pair was happy now. And despite Snow's doubts during the wedding itself, it didn't look like there were any problems in paradise. At least not yet. He was happy for them, even if that wasn't the path that Snow planned on taking.

Especially after what had happened with Kirsten.

"None, but that's not why I'm here."

"Okay." Snow had assumed his friend happened to be walking by his office and decided to pop in. Evidently not. "A patient?"

"No, you, actually."

"Me?" That surprised him. But if the man

was here to tell him their toast had been a big mistake, he was barking up the wrong tree. It may have been a mistake for Kaleb, but it hadn't been a mistake for him.

"My wife actually sent me."

Maybe they were having a barbecue or a get-together and wanted to invite him.

"Okay, what's going on?"

"I think I should be asking you that question."

He frowned. "I don't follow."

Kaleb leaned forward. "You know I don't like sticking my nose in your business, right?"

"Uh, we've been sticking our noses in each other's business ever since we were kids. And I was the one who told you to go after Nicola, wasn't I?"

"Yes, you were. And you were right. Which is why I'm here."

"If you're going to tell me to go after someone, then you've got the wrong friend. There isn't anyone. I mean it."

Kaleb studied him for a minute. "Okay. I believe you." He waited another second or two. "Nicola ran into that new pulmonologist this morning… Dr. Nadif. They're friends. Anyway, she asked Nicola a kind of strange question. She asked what my wife knew about you."

What the hell? He picked up a pen off his blotter and turned it end over end. What had Kirsten told her?

The pediatric nurse's texts came back to mind. Had he read her that wrong?

"Why would she do that?"

One of Kaleb's eyebrows lifted. Great. So now Nicola and Kaleb both knew.

"It was nothing. And I really don't appreciate her going around telling people that we slept together." He stood up. "In fact, I'm going to—"

"Hey, hold on a minute." Kaleb held up a hand, stopping Snow in his tracks. "She's not. In fact, I didn't even know you slept together until this very minute. When *you* told me. Congratulations, by the way. That's exactly how Nicola and I started out."

This was just getting better and better. He dropped back into his chair. So Kirsten hadn't blurted out the truth…he had. But what else would he have thought?

"Sorry to disappoint you, but it was a spur-of-the-moment thing. It meant nothing."

So why were Kirsten's scared eyes branded onto his soul? It was the fact that she hadn't balked at anything they'd done. Not even when some of their foreplay had been passionate enough to sting. Because she'd dished out as much as she'd gotten. And there'd been no fear. No hesitation. It had been sexy and exciting, and he'd been imagining it happening again, even as she stood in front of his door the next morning wearing nothing but a smile. Except that smile had changed the second she tried to open the door.

Dammit!

"That's what I once said, too, Snow. But that's neither here nor there."

Which brought them back to the reason for his friend's visit. "So if she didn't tell Nicola about last night, then what?"

"She asked why your office door has an extra lock on it when no one else's does. She said she went around and looked just to be sure."

So he was right. It had bothered her every bit as much as he thought it had. "What did Nicola tell her?"

"Well, contrary to what you think, I haven't told my wife everything about when we were kids. It never came up. She knows we're friends and that you spent a lot of time at my house, but as far as some of the rest of it…"

"You could have told her. It's no big secret." Except it was. To him. And Snow was glad his friend hadn't said anything. He could only imagine the look of pity that would cross people's faces if they learned about his past. Or wondered if Snow might somehow perpetuate the cycle of abuse.

"It's not my story to tell. But Nicola thought maybe you should know about Dr. Nadif's question."

"Yeah, Kirsten asked me about it, too, and I avoided answering. I've already decided I need to say something to her." He dragged his fingers through his hair. "She got up this morning after we… Well, she found the door to the bedroom locked and got kind of weirded out."

Weirded out was one way to put it.

"You are kind of over the top as far as security goes."

"Yeah, I know. But I always figured it was my business. That it didn't affect anyone else."

His friend studied him. "And Theresa?"

"Well, even without the locks, that was probably destined to fail."

The locks were a symptom of something deeper. Snow was no psychiatrist, but even he understood that.

"I think you're probably right. I just don't want Dr. Nadif causing problems for you. You're a damn good doctor, Snow, but rumors—true or not—can twist things to make them seem far bigger than they actually are."

Yes, they could. He knew that from his experience with that nurse. And he could see how this could be made to look like something it wasn't. "Thanks for the heads-up. I'll talk to her."

"Good." Kaleb stood up. "You don't have to tell her everything. But you do need to explain enough to make her understand."

"I will."

They said their goodbyes, and Snow closed the door behind his friend, leaning against it, but not locking it. Why had Kirsten not just come to his office to ask him about it directly instead of going to Nicola? Well, she probably thought that his friend's

wife knew more than she did. And he could
see that it might be hard for her to come and
ask him. After all, she'd already tried twice.
Once when she'd asked about his lock on his
office. And then again last night, when he'd
evaded the elephant in the room, stepping
around it and trying to pretend it didn't exist.
Kind of hard when she was staring right at it.

So he wasn't going to wait until tomorrow
to talk to her. He was going to have this out
now. Before she asked anyone else besides
Nicola.

He picked up his phone and found her
number. His thumb hovered over the call
button for a second or two before he finally
took a deep breath and mashed it. It rang
twice, and then Kirsten picked up. "Hello?"

He didn't want to go into the fact that
Kaleb had come to his office or that he knew
that she'd gone behind his back and asked
Nicola, when she couldn't get any answers
out of him. Instead, he simply said, "Hey, do
you have a few minutes sometime today to
come by my office so we can go over your
patient's chart before I actually see her?"

"Oh, um, yes. I have some time after
lunch, if that works for you."

No hint of them going to eat lunch together. Not that he wanted to or was even going to suggest it. "I do. Say around one o'clock?"

"That sounds…doable."

Her slight hesitation wasn't lost on him. But she didn't mention last night, and he wasn't going to, either. Not over the phone, anyway. Was she afraid to meet in his office? He'd hate it if that was true, but who could he blame for that besides himself? There might not be anything he could do about what had already happened, but he could sure as hell try to change what happened in the future. Starting with giving her a choice of where to meet. "Would you rather we met somewhere else? We can always go sit on one of the benches outside."

"No. Your office will be fine. Besides, it'll be easier to look at her records on an actual computer rather than on one of our phones."

She had a point there. And her response sounded stronger this time. She was more sure of herself.

"Okay, I'll see you here at one, then."

"See you there."

He tossed his phone onto his desk and

leaned back in his chair. What should have been relief wasn't quite there yet. But hopefully that would come. Once he figured out how to broach the subject of what had happened last night and how to tell her enough, while sparing her the gory details of what his childhood had been like. Well, since he hadn't been able to find the fine line that divided the two, he was just going to have to do the best he could and hope like hell that she just forgot about what had happened and moved on to something else.

That little voice in his head reminded him of their conversation at the Statue of Liberty. Repair what was broken while it was still possible, so that there was no need for a transplant. He thought that was still possible, but he'd have to leave that up for Kirsten to decide.

With her computer tucked under her arm, Kirsten walked the distance from the elevator to Snow's office. Nicola hadn't shed much light on his behavior, but then again, Kirsten hadn't wanted to share everything that had happened last night and this morning. It was all too new and raw to do that.

And although she liked her new friend, she didn't want to chance the news of their sleeping together getting around to other people in the hospital. Especially since she was already pretty sure she'd made a huge mistake.

Why?

Was she afraid people might think she was sleeping her way up the ladder? Well, that fear hadn't exactly stopped her from spending the night with the transplant surgeon, had it? And, good or not, that move could prove to be career suicide if it got around. She was still very new at this hospital, and she wanted people to take her seriously. Impulsive decisions like last night didn't exactly lend themselves to inspiring confidence in patients or co-workers. Sure everyone made mistakes, but she'd known it was a mistake before it even happened. And yet she'd done it, anyway.

She knocked on the door.

Half expecting to hear twenty or thirty locks being unlatched, she was surprised when he simply called for her to enter. She did, noting he wasn't at his desk.

"Over here."

She turned her head and saw him sitting

on his sofa, his laptop parked on the glass-topped table in front of him. Shutting the door, she hesitated over the dead bolt. Did he want her to lock it? Leave it alone.

"It's okay, don't worry about it."

Great, he'd read her mind. She moved over to the seating arrangement, wondering how this was going to work if they were sitting on opposite sides of the table. So she perched on the very edge of the long sofa and placed her own laptop on the table beside his, then booted it up.

"Hey, before we start, I wanted to talk to you about something. I debated on just letting it go, but I don't want it to interfere with our working relationship."

"If it's about last night, don't worry about it. We can acknowledge it was a mistake that won't happen again." She didn't want to sit here while he dissected everything and then tossed it all in the trash. Ha! Hadn't she done almost that very thing?

"It is about last night, but not in the way you might think." He stopped, as if searching for how to begin. "You asked me yesterday about my parents."

Why did he want to talk about that, when

it had nothing to do with what they'd done? "It's okay, you don't need to—"

"I do, because I don't want you to have the wrong idea about something." He shifted so that he was facing her. "I told you I don't have any contact with my dad, and I don't. Because he's in prison."

Shock filled her, knocking away any additional words she might have tossed out about mistakes and what had happened last night. "I'm sorry, Snow. I didn't know. I shouldn't have asked that question."

"Yes, you should have. We ask people all the time about where they're from, whether they have any siblings…what their parents do for a living. You can see how that might be a hard question for me to answer. Because when my dad wasn't drinking or doing drugs, he was using my mom as a punching bag."

Horror filled her. She'd thought all kinds of things. Even thought maybe he was in the witness protection program or something. But none of it came close to the reality of what he was telling her.

"Oh, God. I—I had no idea." Everything fell into place in an instant, and she felt awful for thinking it was Snow who had something to hide. That he had something to be ashamed of. She had a feeling he felt both of those things, though, and her heart ached for him. She felt awful for going to ask Nicola about him.

"I know. I don't tell very many people about it. Kaleb knows because we grew up together, and because I rode my bike to his house during the worst of it."

His bike. She pictured Snow as a little boy pedaling as fast as he could, his fear propelling him to find safety. She swallowed past a knot of emotion that threatened to turn into tears. Tears he probably wouldn't appreciate.

"You were young when this started?"

"Yep. He's my actual birth father, not a stepfather or boyfriend who came along later. And he was there the whole time I was growing up." He shrugged. "You saw some of the residual junk from my past last night. You just didn't realize what you were looking at."

"The locks." She felt like such an idiot. All that talk about whether someone was after him or wondering if he was hiding some kind of nefarious activity. He had been. But he was hiding himself. Not because he was using drugs or had any kinky habits.

"Yes. When I was about seven, my mom came home from work and found me crying. My dad hadn't hit me. Not that time. But he'd come close, and I was scared. Anyway, my mom installed a lock on my bedroom door to help keep me safe."

Did he even know how that sounded? How could a mom leave her child in that kind of situation? Then again, she couldn't see inside the woman's head to see what her reasoning was. Maybe she couldn't get away. Or maybe she had no support system to help her. No one to turn to.

"But he's in prison now, you said."

"Yes. He is. But old habits die hard." He propped his ankle on his knee. "That first lock didn't keep my dad out, but when I was a teenager, I got a job at a locksmith and learned all about how they worked—how to install my own. I worked my way from simple to complicated, until I found a lock that included a steel bar that when turned fitted into a hole on the floor and top of the door frame. I realized I couldn't leave, because then my mom would be all alone. So

I did my best to protect her. And me. Using locks."

"He's in jail now, so your mom must have turned him in."

"No, that was me, when my mom ended up spending a month in ICU. I told the police everything. Testified at his trial."

She couldn't imagine how hard that must have been. How heartbreaking for him and his mom. "How old were you when that happened?"

"I was seventeen and about ready to graduate from high school. I stayed with Kaleb and his family to avoid going through the foster-care system." He sighed. "So the locks became a habit. A symbol of safety and freedom. But more than that, I like installing them. And, yes, there's a neurotic element to it. I no longer *need* them. But they brought me comfort during a hard time in my life. And that's hard to let go of."

His eyes met hers. "I am very sorry, Kirsten, if I scared you by locking the door to my bedroom last night. I hope you know I would never knowingly hurt you, or anyone."

"I do." She decided to be honest. "It took

me by surprise, and I'll admit a lot of thoughts ran through my head before I discarded each of them. I wondered if you were in the witness protection program or something."

"That's why you asked me if someone was after me."

"Yes." She'd also wondered if something from his past had been chasing him. Evidently it was—it just wasn't a physical presence.

"Feel better?"

She did about the reasons for the extra security, but not about why he had it. "I have to confess something. I'm embarrassed about it now."

"Okay."

"I asked Nicola about you. I didn't tell her about last night, but I did ask if she knew anything about you. About why your office door has a lock when no one else's does."

"It's okay. Kaleb already came to see me this morning to ask what was going on. He told me about Nicola. But I'd already decided to talk to you before he showed up at my office door. I was just going to wait until tomorrow to do it. It made me decide that I needed to address it sooner and not give you the watered-down version I'd planned on."

"So you didn't ask me to come here to talk about my patient?"

"I do. It just wasn't my only reason for meeting you today. And it kills two birds with one stone."

"Don't other women wonder why you have extra locks?"

He chuckled. "Well, maybe, but there haven't been that many and they've never actually come out and asked before. No one else knows the whole story, except for Kaleb, obviously, but not too many others outside of my family."

Not even his ex-wife? Not that she was going to ask that kind of question.

So she was the first casual acquaintance he'd given this explanation to? Well, she had kind of freaked out about it, so maybe the other women he'd been with had been cooler about the whole situation.

Well, starting now, she was going to become one of those "cool" women. As glad as she was that he'd told her about his past—and as horrified as she was by what he'd gone through—it didn't change anything.

Last night had been a mistake before his explanation, and it was still a mistake after it.

So no more asking questions or trying to figure him out. Because in the end, it didn't matter. They were colleagues at work and nothing more. The sooner she got that through her thick skull, the better off they both would be.

CHAPTER SEVEN

Snow came into the room and saw a dark-haired preteen flanked by a very worried mom and dad. He and Kirsten had gone over her chart yesterday after the discussion about his parents, and he had to agree with her. It looked like primary pulmonary hypertension might be at the root of the ten-year-old's lung issues.

"Hello, Gretchen, I'm Dr. Tangredi. I understand that you had an MRI done today."

The girl drew a deep breath before coughing into the crook of her elbow several times. The coughing could be due to her lungs, but it also could be a sign that her heart was starting to fail as it struggled to pump oxygen to the far reaches of her body. "Yes, I did. Kirsten thinks it will help us understand what's wrong with me."

He shot the pulmonologist a look. There was a debate in the medical field about whether patients should be encouraged to use a doctor's first name rather than their title. He guessed he knew where Kirsten stood on that particular issue. He found that he kind of liked it—it fit her. And he could see how, in pediatrics especially, it might help young patients connect better with their doctors—how it might take away a little of the fear for them to view their caregivers as people rather than someone who was there to poke and prod them.

"I agree with her. I looked at some of the other tests that have been done. Dr.... I mean Kirsten asked me if I would mind coming in and giving her my opinion."

"She says I might need special care. More than she can give."

"You might." He smiled at her, remembering how Kirsten had said Snow was sometimes a patient's last hope. For some reason, he didn't want to let her down, if that was the case. "Let's wait and see what the results of the MRI are."

Kirsten stepped forward. "We should have them back by Monday."

The hard thing about having tests done on Friday, was that most of the time a doctor had to sign off on them, so not as much happened on the weekends unless it was a life-or-death situation. Gretchen wasn't quite there yet, but she might get there if they couldn't come up with a treatment plan that worked.

Try to repair, so that a transplant isn't needed.

Those words had come back to him a lot in the two days since Kirsten had spent the night. Telling her about his dad had done just that. It hadn't fixed all of the awkwardness between them—that would only happen if and when a time machine came into being so he could go back and undo taking her back to his place. But he did find himself more open emotionally than he had been. Her reaction had been nothing like Theresa's. Kirsten had shown horror, but she had pressed him for more information than he'd been willing to give. And for that he was grateful.

He turned to the child's parents. "So how is she at home?"

"She has a hard time catching her breath,

even walking out to the bus stop in the morning. PE is impossible for her at this point. The school has made a special class in kinesiology just so she doesn't fail her grade. Homeschooling is an option, but she really wants to stay with her friends if she can."

"I can't blame her for that. We'll see what we can do to help her with that. Kirsten says she told you that there might be high blood pressure in the artery that connects Gretchen's lungs with her heart."

"Yes. I've been doing some reading online, but some of what I've found…" Her mom's voice fell away and her eyes filled with tears.

He knew how hard it was to stay strong and not worry about someone you loved more than necessary. He'd done that with his mom more times than he wanted to admit. The times when he was overcome with fear that his dad would kill her. Or him. He'd held all of those emotions in so she wouldn't see it in his eyes.

His glance went to Kirsten and he found her looking at him with…pity?

Oh, hell, no! That was the exact reason he didn't tell people about his past. But in her case he'd had no choice, really. Well, he had had a choice, but the alternative wasn't acceptable to him. Pity was better than fear, right?

He vowed no one would ever need to be afraid of him. And although he knew his demeanor didn't quite reach teddy-bear levels, he hoped he'd kept that promise.

Hoped he would always keep that promise.

"Reading things online is okay, but make sure you get your information from reputable sites, like the big teaching hospitals. And always feel free to ask us anything."

"Okay, thank you. And I do have a question," her dad said. "Is our daughter going to need a transplant someday?"

Well, Snow had said to ask him anything, hadn't he? "Some people with pulmonary hypertension will eventually need a transplant, but some cases can be managed for a long time on medication."

"And Gretchen?"

The child's mom spoke up. "Bob, let's not do this now."

His eyes closed for a second. "You're right. I'm just worried."

"Yes, we both are," she said. "Let's let them get the results of the tests from today, and we'll talk again. Just us."

Snow couldn't have said it better if he tried. And he really didn't want to scare their daughter unnecessarily, so it was probably a discussion they would have just between the grown-ups.

Kirsten smiled at them. "You wouldn't be normal if you weren't worried. But I want you to know we're going to do everything in our power to keep Gretchen as healthy as possible. Maybe even enough to participate in PE within limits."

She'd said "we." Was she including him in that statement? Maybe not, but a warm feeling washed up his chest, anyway, despite the look he'd intercepted earlier. Maybe he'd even imagined it, but he didn't think so.

The girl made a face. "I kind of like learning about muscles."

Kirsten laughed. "Well, that's a good thing. I'll share a secret with you. Kinesiology was one of my favorite subjects in medical school."

"It was?"

She nodded. "Getting to know how so

many things have to come together to get our arm to bend, or our legs to run, is pretty amazing."

Something else that was pretty amazing was watching the way Kirsten came to life when talking to her patient. Yes, she'd been informative and warm when she'd discussed things with Tanya—his patient—but on her own turf, within her own specialty, there was a special confidence that sparkled in her eyes. That sparkle had been missing when she consulted on his case.

"It's cool. We're going to do a project figuring out which muscles help us do what tasks."

The girl had taken three gulps of air in the course of saying that last sentence, a sign that breathing was hard work, and that she was getting tired.

Kirsten must have sensed it, too, because she said, "Well, we'll let you get back to your day. Call me if you have any other questions."

While some doctors might have just said that without giving any real thought as to the actual words, he had a feeling that she knew exactly what she was saying and that she meant it. All of it.

He decided to follow her lead. "Yes, feel free to do the same with me, if you have questions about transplants and the process we use to decide when and if someone needs one."

He pulled out a card from his wallet and handed it to Gretchen's dad, since he was the one who held his hand out for it.

Once they'd said their goodbyes and the family had left the room, Kirsten glanced at him. "Thanks for agreeing to see her."

"Happy to do it."

She touched his hand, stopping where she was. He halted, as well.

"And thank you for telling me about the other thing. I promise I won't share the information with anyone."

He hoped that was true, although she'd asked Nicola about his background. What if someone came to her with the same type of question?

No, he didn't know why, but he believed her. He wanted to think that even if someone tried to pump her for information, she wouldn't share his story without his permission. Unless it was for a very good reason.

"Thanks. I appreciate that. It's not something that comes up in everyday conversation." Actually it had never come up in any conversation before. Except for with Kaleb's family. He still bought his friend's parents gifts for their birthdays and for Christmas. It was the only way he could think of to express his gratitude for them opening their home to a troubled kid. They hadn't known the extent of the abuse, either, until his dad went to prison, and he'd gone to live with them. His mother never talked about it with anyone, and back then, Snow had been afraid that anything he said would just get his mom in trouble with his dad. So being quiet had been his best bet.

She licked her lips, then said, "Maybe you can get rid of the extra locks one at a time."

Not happening. They didn't hurt anyone, and they'd been in his life for a lot longer than she had. Even Theresa had lived with that idiosyncrasy without too many complaints. It had been his lack of ability to connect emotionally that had left her cold.

Well, he wouldn't have to worry about that

with Kirsten. They'd connected on a sexual level, but emotionally? Not so much. There'd been no need. There was still no need.

He decided to keep things vague. "Yeah. Maybe. We'll have to see what happens."

It was one way of saying "forget it, not happening," without actually saying the words.

"Okay. Thanks again. Do you want me to let you know what the MRI results are?"

"Yes, please. I'd like to keep up with the case just in case she does end up needing a transplant, even if it isn't right away. Maybe it won't be as bad as we think."

It was worse than she'd thought.

The right side of Gretchen's heart, as she'd suspected and noticed on X-rays, had disturbing changes. The walls had thickened and the ventricle itself had enlarged in an effort to hold and pump more blood with each beat. But it was already beginning to backfire, causing more strain on a heart muscle that was quickly becoming weary. She needed to call the family and let them know, but first she needed to talk to Snow and get his opinion. Again.

She didn't really want to do it by phone, though. So she headed for his office. Knocking, she noticed the lock was still there. But it wasn't like he could just pull it off and toss it. Taking it off would leave an ugly defect in the wood and would leave space to get a finger or two in that could unlatch the lock on the knob.

The door opened and there stood Snow. "You got the results back this morning, didn't you?"

"Yes. I was hoping you were here. Can we go somewhere to talk? Or are you busy right now?"

He glanced inside his office, but evidently decided—like she had—that meeting in a less private area would be better. "Do you want to go down to the foyer? There are a few seating areas off to the side. Maybe we can snag one of them."

"That's a great idea."

The hospital entryway always impressed her with its towering ceiling and chandelier. And despite its massive size it made everything look…welcoming.

They made their way to the elevator and headed down. And then they were in the busiest area of the hospital, where visitors and patients alike hurried in and out.

Surprisingly, they were able to find a four-chair grouping in one of the far corners of the space and Kirsten sat down, setting her computer in front of her. "So there's probably still the possibility of managing Gretchen's condition with medication, but I want us to be on the same page as far as treatment goes."

They discussed the ins and out of the MRI results and Snow outlined the steps that they would need to do in order to be placed on the transplant list.

"I don't think we're at that point yet, but unless something drastically changes, she'll probably be on it within a year."

"I was thinking the same thing, but wanted to hear your take on everything."

"Do you want me there when you talk to the parents?"

"Yes, if you don't mind, since you can speak to the transplant side of the equation."

He nodded, leaning forward to look at her computer screen as if looking for something they'd missed. "It's not going to be an easy conversation. And I'll have to be honest and tell them that wait times are often horrendous."

"I know all about wait times."

"I know you do." He paused. "Is it hard?"

"Hard?"

"Treating patients who are sometimes in the same position your mom was. Sometimes worse."

"Sometimes." She sighed. Her mom's image still came up from time to time when she was talking to a patient. She wondered if that would ever go away. "It's harder in cases like this, when I know there aren't a whole lot of treatment options to slow the progress and when a transplant is a very real possibility."

Looking at Snow, who still struggled with issues from his past, she imagined he understood more than he realized. His trauma had lasted for a lot longer than hers had.

"What will you do if he gets out of prison?" The question came out before she could stop it.

"Nothing." He didn't ask what she was talking about. It was pretty obvious.

"And if he tries to contact you? Or your mom?"

"I think he knows better than that." Snow's face had taken on a hardness that actually had her worried for his father's safety, as ironic as that was. The boy who'd once needed protection from a monster might pose a threat to that very monster.

"I hope so."

"Sorry, I had no business asking that."

He nudged her shoulder with his. "It's okay. Believe me, I've asked myself that very question for more years than I can count."

"How long is he in for?"

"Twenty. So he still has quite a few years to go. He's been turned down for parole five times in a row."

That made her nervous. "So they still think he's a threat."

"Not very much chance of a man like that changing his stripes."

But people could change. She wasn't sure about people like his dad, but surely a person could change for the better if they really wanted to. If they worked hard, they could exchange their old habits for something better. Something that helped rather than harmed those around them.

Kirsten had changed as a result of her

mom's death. Snow had asked if it was hard. Yes, it was damn hard, but the alternative was to turn her back on what had happened to her mother and pretend people like her didn't exist. She couldn't bring herself to do that.

So here she was in a hospital wing talking about a young girl's fate. At least Kirsten could play a part in advocating for her patient, to help make sure she got what she needed, even if what she needed most was a transplant. Getting her on that list in a timely fashion was crucial to giving her the best possible chance for survival. She was pretty sure Gretchen's parents would agree with her on that.

And if she couldn't make that happen?

She wasn't going to think about that right now. It was why she'd enlisted Snow's help. He knew how the system worked—he'd been playing the game for years.

Except this wasn't a game. It was deadly serious.

She went back to the subject they'd been discussing. "I hope your father leaves you and your mom the hell alone, then."

He looked surprised by the words for a

second, then said, "Don't worry. I'll make sure of that."

By buying more locks for his mom's door? And his? Or by doing something more drastic?

Kirsten did what he'd done earlier and jabbed her shoulder into his arm. "Just make sure you don't wind up in jail yourself. You have a lot of people counting on you." In case he got the wrong idea, she hurriedly added, "Your patients, I mean. And your mom."

He smiled. "I knew what you meant. And don't worry. I made myself a vow a long time ago that I would be nothing like my father."

"From what I can see, you've kept that vow. I'm sure your mom is very proud of the man you've become. You said she lives in Massena? Is that how you pronounce it?"

"Yes, on both counts. It's where Kaleb and I grew up. My dad worked at one of the locks on the Saint Lawrence Seaway."

"Locks?" She had no idea what that was.

He smiled. "It's not like that lock on my bedroom door. It's actually a way that ships can travel between areas of a canal that have different water levels. The boats are held in a watertight box while water either fills or leaves the box until it matches the next stretch of canal. Then it's free to continue on its way."

Her face had heated at the reference to his bedroom, but by the time his explanation was finished, she'd pretty much forgotten about her momentary embarrassment. She was instead fascinated by how the ships moved forward.

"So, in a way, the boxes are a kind of lock. The ship is locked in, right?"

"Hmm...right. I'm not sure what the origin of the word is for this particular kind of lock."

She thought for a few seconds. "I don't know that we even have locks in Lebanon. I've never heard of them before."

"It's an interesting sight. You should try to visit one and see what happens."

"Maybe I will." It was one more thing to add to what she wanted to do before leaving the country. *If* she left. The thought of that wasn't quite as appealing as it once was. Because of Snow?

God, she hoped not. And she still had a

while before she'd have to let the hospital know, if she decided to go that route. She'd also have to let her dad know so they could try to find a hospital that would accept her credentials. And although Arabic was her mother tongue, she'd learned a lot of technical words in English. She wasn't sure she knew what they all were in Arabic. Maybe she should start trying to review them.

She snapped the lid on her laptop closed. "I'll call Gretchen's parents and set up the meeting. Is there a time that's better for you?"

"I'll check." He opened his phone and scrolled through what must be his calendar. "I have patients to meet with the first part of the week, and, of course, if an organ comes available, I can't always promise I won't be in surgery."

"I know." She had a thought, since she was thinking about researching things for her possible move. "I'd really like to observe transplant surgery being done at NYC Memorial, if that's possible."

"Thinking of changing fields?"

"No. I'm pretty happy where I am. But it would be nice to actually see what goes on, so that I can explain things to my patients a little bit better. Especially if you're not around to help me do that."

"That makes sense." He studied his phone for another minute or two. "I have two patients that are close to the top of the list and are just waiting on an organ to be found. How about if I call you before the next one goes into surgery, and if you're free, you can come observe."

Excitement bubbled in her system. Because of the possibility of watching, not because it was Snow. "Really?"

"Yes, Really. I have one heart transplant patient and one heart-lung patient on my list."

"Thank you." There was something bittersweet in watching something that her mom had missed out on. But she liked to think that her mother would approve, if she knew. And it would be one more way that she could empathize and relate to her patients.

He stood. "Well, I'd probably better get back to work, but let me know when you schedule the meeting with Gretchen's parents and I'll do my best to be there, how's that?"

"That is all I can ask. Thank you again."

"You're welcome, Kirs. Happy to do it."

The shortening of her name made her throat tighten. Her mom had called her that. In fact, she was the last person to have called her Kirs. If anyone else had tried, she probably would have set them straight in a hurry, but somehow with Snow, it sounded natural. Right. She wasn't even sure he was aware that he'd done it. But she liked it.

"I'll see you later, then."

"Yes, see you."

He turned and walked away. Kirsten watched as he headed down the corridor, his steps firm and confident, his lanky form looking like he hadn't a care in the world.

She knew differently, though. He did have a care. Lots of them, in fact. And she wasn't sure that the man who had so many locks on his doors didn't have an equal number of them on his heart.

CHAPTER EIGHT

Snow had gotten a call that a heart had become available for his heart patient three hours ago. It had just arrived, in fact, from a different part of New York. The team was getting everything ready in the surgical suite and he'd already met with the family. He checked in with Kirsten.

"I'm looking at around thirty minutes as a start time. Can you make it?"

"Yes, just tell me which suite and I'll be there."

He double-checked the number for the operating room. "Looks like it's number four. I'm heading down in a minute to scrub in."

"Okay, see you there."

He quickly reviewed the patient's chart, reminding himself of the game plan as he took the elevator to the surgical area. Then, scrubbing his arms with a little more vigor than necessary, he tried to figure out why he'd agreed to let Kirsten observe. But it would have appeared strange if he'd said no to her, when really, any of the staff with enough interest were usually allowed to watch as long as the surgeon agreed. There were only one or two who preferred to keep a "closed" surgery, one in which no one outside of surgical staff was allowed to watch. For those few, they usually stated that they wanted no distractions, and usually no music in the room.

Snow was also a no-music guy, although he wasn't as much of a hard ass about observers. The only time he'd closed a surgery that he could remember had been at the wishes of a patient who hadn't wanted anyone except for necessary staff to see her unclothed. He'd respected her wishes.

His arms still wet, he pushed through the doors to the surgical suite with his shoulder, then dried his hands with the provided sterile towels, finishing his routine. There was always an air of anticipation and nerves as he got ready to operate. There would be no second chances, if he made a mistake.

Unlike lungs or other organs, the heart was especially difficult, because if it refused to start, there was no going back, no fix, and the patient would die on his operating table. So far, every donor heart had cooperated with him. But he knew that with each surgery, the odds were growing that there would be a first time.

His gaze headed to the observation area, despite his admonitions to avoid glancing over. And just like Kirsten had said, she was there. She gave a little wave, which he acknowledged with a nod in her direction.

He again wondered about her being there. But why? Why her in particular? Was it because they'd slept together? Because she knew why he locked himself in his bedroom?

Actually, maybe that's why she *should* be here. So she could see that he was as normal as any other surgeon. He wasn't sure why that was so important, but it was.

He turned back to his team, which was already in place. "Is everything ready?"

The heart was there in its special container and the patient was already sedated and ready. They were just waiting on him.

He nodded for the recorder to be turned on and gave his initial remarks, including the patient's name, age and diagnosis. "Ready to begin."

The instruments were already placed in order of use on sterile trays and the surgical nurse was there, waiting on his first request.

They washed the patient's chest with surgical scrub and put the drape in place.

The first part of the surgery went like clockwork—he opened the chest and spread the ribs, exposing a heart that was enlarged and weakened by cardiomyopathy. There'd been no way to fix this heart, no medication that could reverse the disease process, just short-term patches geared toward getting the patient to this point in the transplant process. He took note of the implanted defibrillator and planned the timing of removing it. Everything had to be done in a methodical order. One mistake…

Damn. He needed to stop this before it became a self-fulfilling prophecy. He could feel Kirsten's eyes on him, even though she wasn't in the room. But none of that mattered. The only thing that counted was the patient, who was depending on him for life. For a fresh start. Someday that patient might be ten-year-old Gretchen, her family sitting in some waiting room hoping and praying that their daughter made it out of surgery alive.

He pulled his attention fully back on his patient. Preparing her for bypass was one of the most critical stages of the surgery, and he was well aware that he was about to take a beating heart and shut it off forever. Essentially, he was playing God. There was a scary solemnity to the act, and he paused for a second or two as he always did and weighed the risks and benefits. But this first actual look at the diseased heart proved what the MRI, EKGs and biopsy had told him. It was dying and carrying his patient down the river with it. It had reminded him of his dying marriage and the need to sever the link before it sucked both he and Theresa down with it. It had been the right decision.

And Kirsten? Was this the right decision? Yes, because he was simply letting her observe, not marrying her.

"Getting ready for bypass." He glanced at

the perfusionist, who was sitting at a board, adjusting knobs and sliding relays. The man nodded at him. Okay, it was now or never.

With the tubing attached to the aorta and the vena cava, he shifted the job of oxygenating blood over to the machine.

"We're good," the perfusionist said.

Danny's job was as nerve-racking as his. Set up behind a table of controls, he looked almost like someone sitting at a mixing board at a recording studio. And maybe it was similar. And although it had nothing to do with sound, he had to get the levels perfect to give the patient the best chance at surviving. Maybe relationships were like that. If one element was out of whack, it could mean death. Or if one body part started to fail, it could mean the same thing.

Time to disconnect the heart.

Snow worked on detaching the organ from the patient, putting it in the stainless-steel specimen tray. A nurse whisked it away. Halfway there. He glanced at the clock. Two hours—right on time.

He sucked down a cleansing breath and clenched his fists twice, a habit he'd gotten into as he prepared for the second stage of his surgery—placing the donor heart into the patient. He'd already examined the heart once, but he gave it another pass as he got ready to put it in the chest cavity. He carefully reconnected it, and allowed the blood supply to flow through the tissues. Sometimes that was all that was needed to start the heart beating again.

Not this time.

It was okay. Sometimes the technique worked and sometimes it needed a little extra push.

"Paddles." The nurse handed the small unit to him and charged them to the correct specifications. Saying a quick prayer over the donor heart, he laid the paddles on either side of the heart.

"Clear!"

Snow sent the electrical charge through the organ and it spasmed, then was still.

Hell! Not what he wanted to see. A jolt of fear went through him and he tamped it down, then he placed the paddles a second time on the heart and shocked it. Stared at it. Willed it to come back to life in its new home.

It did. With big steady pumps that replaced

the shallow strained movements of his patient's old heart. He closed his eyes for a second, sheer thankfulness spearing through him. Another life, saved. The energy in the room turned electric as the team began excitedly talking among themselves for a few seconds before settling back in to focus on the final stage of surgery.

He double-checked all of his sutures, looking for any and all leaks that might compromise the patient once they left this room. Finding none, he prepared to close the chest cavity. Sternal wires were used to put the sternum back together, and while some heart surgeons still used sutures or staples to close the surgical incision, Snow actually preferred glue, finding it made for a better scar.

And after that… Well, Kirsten was still up there, so he'd have to go speak to her once he was done, as well as the patient's family. But right now, his mood was one of elation, something he felt each time he had a successful surgery. It had been a little over four hours, and he was tired. But it was the good kind of tired. While his team sometimes went out for celebratory drinks, Snow rarely joined them. He preferred to sit in the dark of his office and unwind. It was one of the times he played music, a kind of "recovery" playlist that he'd made up specifically for surgeries, since he liked to spend the night in his office, in case there were complications.

He'd joined the skin edges together with the glue and left openings for the drainage tubes, so everything held together, just as it should have. He glanced at the monitors. The heart was still going strong. There could be some PVCs and arrhythmias as a result of postsurgical inflammation, but they'd keep a close eye on the patient for several days.

A long gauze bandage was applied over the incision to keep things as clean as possible and to protect the site.

"Okay, that about wraps it up. Good work, everyone. Let's hope for an excellent outcome."

Snow waited until the patient was wheeled out of the operating room and headed to recovery before he removed his gloves and surgical gown. Only then did he look up at Kirsten and motion for her to meet him outside the room.

He wasn't sure why, but he was suddenly glad he'd allowed her to watch. He had a few friends, but they were all in different fields. But from watching the way she dealt with Tanya, his earlier patient, and with Gretchen, she'd probably been holding her breath, too, when he'd tried to get that donor heart started.

Kirsten was waiting for him when he pushed through the door. She smiled. "That was…amazing. Truly amazing. But I can honestly say, I do not envy you your job. I don't think I could handle the tension of trying to start a heart and honestly not knowing if it will beat."

"It can be nerve-racking, no doubt. But every field has its own pressures. You just learn to deal with it." He nodded toward the hallway. "Want to walk with me so I can let the family know how things went?"

"Isn't that something you'd rather do alone?"

"If you need to leave, I'll understand. I just thought we could grab some coffee or something."

"I'd like that." They walked down the corridor while Kirsten's animated voice recounted all the things about the surgery that she'd found interesting. Now that the initial euphoria had worn off, Snow was feeling a bone-dragging tiredness that came from hours of double-checking each step before he actually performed it. From the adrenaline that had been pumping through his system nonstop to the sudden cessation of the hormone, he swung back toward the low end of the spectrum. Kirsten's voice was actually helping slow the fall in some weird way, becoming a buoy that kept him from being sucked too far down.

He went into the waiting room and a small group of people rose from their spots, the fear on their faces clear. He smiled at them before he ever reached them.

"Oh, God, she's okay, then?" The woman's husband, Mr. Fisher, was the first to speak.

"She did very well. Everything went as expected." No need to say the heart hadn't started right away. That happened from time to time, since the organ had had a shock of its own.

Chaos erupted as family members hugged each other, some laughing, some crying as they all coped in different ways. He understood their reactions all too well. He'd had his own ways of coping. He still did, although the biting fear of abuse was long gone. He glanced at Kirsten to make sure she was still there.

She was. He wasn't sure why he'd suggested coffee. But he really wanted some. Wanted to drink it in his office to decompress. With her. Normally he preferred doing that alone with just his playlist going softly in the background. He'd sip at his coffee and kick up his feet, thinking of just…nothing. The after-surgery ritual was so strongly ingrained, he could feel it before it even happened.

"I'm going to go back and check on her in a moment. Once she's awake enough—" he nodded at her husband "—you can go back to see her for just a few minutes. Right now, what she needs the most is rest. But her new heart is working very well. It's strong, and her oxygen levels are great for a change. She should start feeling a whole lot better once the surgical wounds heal. She even mentioned wanting to do a five-K sometime in the future."

Mr. Fisher's eyes watered. "She loved to

run. Did it every year until her heart started acting up."

"She'll have to be careful for a while, but there's no reason she can't take up running again." He patted the man's shoulder. "They'll come and get you as soon as she's ready for a visitor."

"Thank you. For everything. She would be dead without you."

"She has a strong will to live. That's what kept her going long enough to get the transplant."

He said his goodbyes and went back through the same door. He turned to Kirsten, who had been quiet through the exchange. "Ready for that coffee?"

"Yes. But if you don't want me to stay, I'll understand. I know some surgeons like to go off by themselves for a while."

"I'm normally one of them, but I could really use some company right now."

"Are you sure?"

"I am. If you're okay going back to my office, that is. A whole cafeteria full of chaotic conversations isn't exactly what I had in mind."

She hesitated.

Hell, maybe she thought he wanted something besides company. Or the lock incident had her nervous about spending time with him. "We can go somewhere else, if you'd prefer. I promise, all I want is someone to sit with."

"No, it's not that… Your office is fine. Or mine. Either one."

"Let's do mine, then." He wasn't sure why, but he needed to be on familiar turf right now. Just a place that he knew and understood.

"How about if I grab our coffees while you check on your patient. I'll meet you back at the office."

"I would really appreciate that." More than she knew. "I just take mine black."

She smiled. "Yeah. I remember from our trip to the Statue of Liberty."

That seemed like ages ago, but it wasn't. It had been less than a week ago.

He made a quick trip to Recovery, where his patient was awake, but groggy from pain meds and the aftereffects of anesthesia. And was still intubated at the moment.

"You did really well, Marilyn. I just talked to your husband about the possibility of you running a five-K. I told him that's a very real possibility now." The woman squeezed his hand to show she understood. "I'll come back by in the morning, okay? Your husband will be here in a little bit to see you. But we need to make sure you get some rest."

Then he was headed back to his office. Kirsten was already standing outside the door, holding two disposable cups with heat sleeves wrapped around each. "I hope you haven't been waiting long."

"Nope. Just got here." She handed him a cup. "Nothing but straight coffee in there."

"Thanks." Snow unlocked the lock on the knob, then, conscious of her eyes on him, he turned the key in the dead bolt. Then the door swung open, and he waited for her to go inside.

"Do you mind if I play some music?" Of course, that could be taken the wrong way, too. "It's on a loop that I run through, every time I do surgery."

"It's fine. How about I take one of the chairs, and you can stretch out on your sofa. You look exhausted."

"It's been a long day," he admitted. "I'll try not to fall asleep on you."

She frowned and stood just inside the door. "Are you sure you wouldn't rather be alone and take a nap?"

"Like I said, it would be nice to have company. As long as you don't mind staying."

"Of course not. I'll be happy to." She came fully into the room. "And if you do happen to fall asleep, I'll just let myself out."

He nodded, then went over to his computer and cued up his playlist. Soft jazz filled the space, the sound of a saxophone pouring over him. Sighing, he sat on the sofa, took a sip of his coffee and then held it on his thigh. When she sat down on a nearby chair, she was concentrating on something, her head tilted.

"What?" he asked.

"Your music. I like jazz," She said. "The Ohio Jazz Festival was one of the last places I went with my mom. It was very different, and we thought we'd just go to see what the music was like. We both ended up loving it. It was very different from anything we'd ever heard before. I went on a listening binge when we got home."

That surprised him. People either liked

jazz or they didn't. There wasn't much in between. "I find it relaxing."

They sat for a few minutes in silence. He could feel his muscles beginning to unwind, the cramps working their way out of his fingers. One of the reasons he sat in his office rather than going home was because Theresa used to talk incessantly the second he arrived, even when he was so tired he could barely focus. And she expected him to carry his share of the conversation.

Yet, Kirsten seemed to instinctively know he needed quiet. He wasn't even sure why he'd invited her back here, but he was now glad he had.

And when she kicked off her shoes and curled into a corner of her chair, head leaning on the back cushion, he couldn't quite take his eyes off of her. She made his heart do all kinds of things. But right now she made him feel restful.

She looked like she was totally into the music. Was barely moving, except to put one arm under her head. "Would you rather have the sofa?"

She didn't answer, so he looked closer and noted the slow rise and fall of her chest, the way she seemed totally at peace. It was then he realized he needn't be worried about falling asleep in front of her. Because she'd just fallen to sleep in front of him.

Sleep had never been further from his mind at the moment. All he wanted to do was sit and watch her, a strange longing singing through his veins that seemed to match the plaintive tones of the saxophone.

When he'd finished telling her about his father earlier, he'd felt a relief greater than any he could remember, and wasn't sure he'd ever feel again. And afterward, she hadn't avoided him or talked a mile a minute as if needing to fill every gap of silence, for fear he might bring up his past again.

No, he'd caught a few glances that he thought might be pity, but he hadn't been convinced of that. And she definitely hadn't balked at coming back to his office. Or falling asleep in front of him.

So with a sigh, he set down his coffee on the table and stretched out on the sofa, turning on his side so that he could continue to watch her.

And as he did, something stole over him that he hadn't felt in a very long time: a sense of peace and rightness. Rightness in her being here. Rightness in confiding in her, even though he still wasn't sure why he had.

He wasn't sure what he was going to do about it, but that was a decision that didn't need to be made today. Or even tomorrow.

So for right now, he was content to simply lie on this couch and simply…be.

CHAPTER NINE

KIRSTEN CAME TO with a start. Blinking, she tried to pull her brain back from wherever it had been. Music played in the background, and she wasn't sure exactly where she…

Her eyes landed on the sofa and found Snow there, eyes open, watching her.

"Wow, I'm sorry. I was supposed to be keeping you company, not snoring away in your chair." Her eyes flashed to him. "I wasn't snoring…was I?"

One side of his mouth quirked up. "Do you want the truth, or…"

The thought that her snoring might have kept him awake was mortifying. "I am so sorry. I'll leave so you can—"

"I'm kidding. You didn't snore. But you did make these cute little snuffling sounds."

Her face turned hot. "Did you get any sleep at all?"

"No, but I don't always try to. Sometimes just stretching out in here is enough to get me back where I need to be."

A thought hit her. "Do you normally bring someone back here?" Maybe he didn't like being alone, either. Kind of like she felt about eating at restaurants alone.

"No. It's normally too distracting."

"So you don't find me distracting." She wasn't sure whether to be flattered or insulted. Especially since seeing him lying flat out on that sofa was beginning to distract her. A lot. It brought back some memories of their night together. It was funny how that was now such a blur. Oh, the remembered sensations were there. In fact, they were doing a number on her now, but the actual events were just bits and pieces of them moving in time with each other, of straining toward the other, of…

And she needed to stop thinking about that.

"I think you know that's not true." As if he'd read her thoughts and needed to change the subject, he sat up. "So what did you think of surgery? I didn't get a chance to ask you much after the fact, since I needed to go talk to her relatives."

"Like I said, it was amazing. I knew the mechanics of it, but to see the damaged heart actually being lifted out of someone's body is a little disconcerting."

"It is. I think about that every time I do one of these. It's like I'm putting something to death."

"Sometimes in order to save something, you have to sacrifice something else. Something that is causing harm and might even result in death."

"I hadn't really thought about it like that. But it makes sense in a lot of areas and not just medicine."

Was he thinking of his dad? How he'd had to sacrifice him, in order to stop him from harming his mom?

"It's the right thing to do in those cases."

He met her eyes. "That doesn't always make it any easier."

"I imagine it doesn't. But if you choose to do nothing, then aren't you guilty of sitting back and allowing it to happen?"

His jaw tightened. "Yes, I guess you are.

And sometimes you wished you'd intervened a lot sooner, and wonder if maybe you could have prevented—"

"Stop." She got up and went over to the sofa to sit next to him, putting her hand on his. There was no doubt what they were talking about now. "You were a kid. Making those kinds of decisions shouldn't have been left up to you. The fact that you were willing to do it at all… Well, you probably saved your mom's life. Who knows what would have happened the next time?"

She was sure he'd had this same kind of argument with himself time and time again.

"Those locks, Snow. I'm pretty sure you have PTSD from what your dad did, from what your mom went through."

This time he didn't say anything. She wasn't sure if he disagreed with her, or if he simply didn't want to talk about it. She couldn't blame him.

She put her hand on his cheek, turning his head until he was looking at her. "Please don't take that the wrong way. I can't imagine having to do what you did. I think you were impossibly brave. And you didn't back down, even though it meant your dad was going to prison. You asked someone to re-move what was killing your family and to take it where it couldn't do any more harm. As a transplant surgeon, you of all people should get that analogy. You have to re-move the cause in order to fix the problem. Maybe you went into transplant surgery for that very reason, without realizing it. Just like I went into pulmonology because of my mom."

He reached up and stroked her hair, a mus-cle working in his cheek. "You're pretty in-credible, you know that?"

"I'm really not."

"I beg to differ." He leaned down and placed a light kiss on her mouth that made her want to curl her hands into his shirt and pull him closer. "And I think you're right. And you know what, it helps looking at it like that."

She smiled. "I'm glad. Because I think you're pretty incredible yourself."

"Do you?"

She nodded.

This time when he kissed her, it wasn't just some quick peck on the lips. It was a slow, drawn-out kiss that wound its way through her. Unhurried. Unwavering. Bringing with it a hum of emotion that she hadn't felt in quite a while.

She inched closer to him and cupped his face, wishing she could heal the hurt that he'd been put through all those years ago. But, of course, she couldn't. So she settled for showing him in the only way she knew how that she admired his bravery, his willingness to stay in a situation that wasn't of his making in order to try to protect his mom.

And she did admire him. In so many ways. She wasn't sure when that had come about or why, but she cared about him.

There wasn't much time to dwell on that realization, though, because the kiss was deepening. His hands were beginning to wander as need erupted between them all over again.

And this time, Kirsten didn't want to take the time to go back to one of their apartments—she wanted him right here in this room, in the midst of the intimacy that was floating through the air. It seemed like a just conclusion to their conversation.

She found his shirt buttons with her fingers and undid them one at a time, pushing the garment away so she could touch his skin. God, she loved the feel of him.

Snow wrapped his arms around her and laid her back on the sofa, pressing her into the soft leather cushions. He surrounded her, his solid weight warm and welcome as he continued to kiss her. He lifted up enough to push up her skirt, and with her help, they soon had it bunched around her waist.

"I want you so much."

The heated words rumbled against her throat and matched everything she felt inside. She didn't care what the consequences were. Didn't care where they found themselves tomorrow. Right now, she just wanted him inside of her. In more ways than one.

She felt more than saw him taking out his wallet and retrieving a condom, heard the snick of his zipper being lowered.

Oh, God, this was going to happen.

And she wanted it. Wanted it more than she'd wanted anything in her life. She was ready when he pushed aside her underwear and found her, sliding home in a rush.

She gasped, the incredible fullness feeling familiar and new at the same time.

She wrapped her legs around his waist, the fabric of his pants adding an element of sexiness as it rubbed against her inner thighs with each movement of his hips. He intoxicated her. Thrilled her. Made her want to stay with him forever.

When one hand slid under her shirt and found her breast, his thumb brushing over the peak, she remembered the way he'd brushed it over his steering wheel. How she'd longed to feel it on her skin. That trip seemed like forever ago.

She closed her eyes and let the sensations wash over her and through her, absorbing it into her brain. And her heart.

His movements weren't frantic, but there was a contagious intensity to him that pulled her along with him through space and time. She touched his face, tracing the planes of his cheeks, and when he lifted his head to look at her, she brushed her index finger along his lips. He opened and captured it, sucking it deeper, his tongue sliding along it in a way that brought an ecstasy of its own.

"Ah…" She couldn't remain silent, couldn't prevent herself from whimpering as nerve endings awoke and were teased and tantalized to the breaking point.

And when his hand edged between their bodies to find her, she pushed closer, head going back as the pressure grew, needing him so much. So very much.

Then like a dam bursting, the raging torrent inside of her broke free, and she gave a loud keening cry as pleasure crashed over her, dragging her along with it. Snow bit down on her finger as he plunged into her and strained for several long seconds. Then his weight settled back down on her all at once, and he allowed her finger to slide free, saying goodbye with a tiny kiss to its tip. His breath against the side of her neck was hot and unsteady.

"Hell."

She couldn't really think. Couldn't articulate enough to answer whatever his "hell" meant. Maybe he'd meant it was incredibly hot. It had been.

Although something made her wonder…

Then he was up and off her with a speed that shocked her, striding over to the door and turning both the locks.

She realized he'd forgotten to lock the door. She laughed, sat up and tried to straighten her skirt. "It's a little late for that, isn't it?"

He didn't crack a smile, didn't do anything except stand there with this grim look on his face. He could have been peering into the face of death, for all she knew. Except he was staring right at her. A shiver went through her.

"Snow?"

"Anyone could have come in here and found us."

The way he said that...

She yanked her shirt back down over her breasts, even as he disposed of his condom and zipped himself back in. Something was wrong. This wasn't just about the unlocked door.

"But they didn't."

He didn't respond, but she felt him withdrawing emotionally, like one of those motion pictures of an erupting volcano that, when rewound, shows everything being sucked back into the fissure before closing it up tight. As if nothing had ever happened.

Okay, so he evidently viewed this as one more mistake. Like the night they'd spent together. Only this time it wasn't the locks that bothered her, it was his behavior.

She swallowed. He reminded her of Dave, who had walked away from their relationship as it was dying on the ground. Or of that doctor who had given her mom the bad news about her condition being terminal. A total emotional detachment. That man had felt nothing for her mom, nothing for her family's pain. Or if he did, not a glimmer of it showed.

That's why Snow looked at her like she was death incarnate. Because he was about to do what he did with all of his transplant patients. Like he'd done with his father. He was going to remove her from his life, just like he did a diseased heart or a set of lungs.

You were never in his life in the first place, Kirsten.

Emotions had been high, and the sex had just happened. And Snow regretted it. It was there in his face, in the hands that were balled into fists.

Pain speared through her, although she

wasn't sure why. They meant nothing to each other.

Except that wasn't true. She'd been scrabbling around trying to grab on to an emotion right before they fell onto the couch together. And now, when she looked into her heart, she realized she'd succeeded in capturing it…was still holding on tight to it.

She loved him.

Horrified, she tried to release the emotion back into the universe, but it had already grown long tendrils that had wrapped themselves in and through her heart, refusing to release it.

Snow still hadn't said anything and panic was beginning to well up inside of her. He'd not only locked everyone out of the room, but he'd also locked them in. Together.

Well, she was going to save him the trouble of making up reasons why they couldn't see each other anymore or how this was a big mistake—which for him, it obviously was. And she wasn't going to text him or ask him why, like she'd done with Dave.

Walking over to him, she looked into his face. His eyes were back to the way they'd been when they'd first met.

Cool, unreachable.

Inside, that invasive plant that had taken over her heart was telling her to beg him to talk to her, to give them a chance. But why? They'd had sex on two occasions. Two. That was nothing in most people's books. And it certainly didn't add up to a relationship. Besides, she'd kind of been through this once before. The excuses. The emotional pulling back. And if you had to beg someone to let you into their life…

Well, it just wasn't worth it. So here she went…

"Hey, we may not agree on much, but I think we can both agree that this was a mistake, and I'm sorry. I swore to myself that it would never happen again after that first night." That was all true. But here came the part where she'd have to fudge things a little bit. "But here's where I give you an easy out. You were right about something. I *am* leaving NYC Memorial. It may not be tomorrow or next week, but it's going to be soon. Maybe even within a month or two. I'll be moving back to Lebanon to be with my dad…my family. So as soon as I wrap up my current caseload, I'll be out of your hair. No one will be the wiser."

The look of relief that crossed his face wasn't her imagination, and it sent another stab of pain through her.

"So you're leaving. I thought you said you weren't."

"Not exactly. What I said was 'who knows where I'll be in a year's time.' I wanted on at NYC Memorial to see if there were any cutting-edge lung treatments I could take back with me to Lebanon when I went. I wasn't sure when I came how long I would be here. But I'm thinking shorter is better at this point."

"Do *not* leave because of what we just did."

It would be hard to respond to that with anything that was less than a lie. Even if he hadn't turned into something as stiff and lifeless as that statue they'd visited in the harbor, her plans still included moving back to Lebanon. So wasn't this better in the end? If she'd loved him and he reciprocated, that choice would be so much harder. But thankfully he'd made it easy, had confirmed that what she was doing was the right thing. "Like

I said, my plans were always to go back. I miss my father, and the rest of my family."

He probably wouldn't challenge that, because he wouldn't be able to relate to a person actually having a father worth missing.

She realized the jazz that had been softly playing in the background was still going. Except the music didn't seem soothing anymore. It seemed mournful, and unbearably sad. But it was definitely fitting for saying this particular goodbye. And the hole he was going to leave was so much bigger than what Dave had left her with. She only hoped it would heal, given enough time.

He was blocking her exit, and if he didn't move, she was going to do something she regretted. Like cry in front of him.

"If you'll just unlock the door, I'll let you get back to your day." She forced a smile. "I'm glad your surgery went well."

He didn't say anything, just went over to the door and turned both of the locks, making a way for her to escape.

And that's what she did. With as much dignity and grace as she could muster. And then she was out of his office and would soon be out of his life.

* * *

As soon as she was gone, Snow went over to his desk and sat down behind it, turning off the music so he could have peace and quiet. It didn't work, because there was still a cacophony of noise going on inside of him that refused to be silenced. Kirsten's name was on a loop that repeated again and again and again.

What the hell had he done? He should have said something to her, should have been the one to apologize. Instead, he'd let her walk out of that door without a single damn word. Without a single argument.

She may have been planning to leave all along, like she'd said, but he could almost guarantee that the timing had changed because of what had happened in this room.

He'd overreacted about the locks. He knew he had. But when he realized he hadn't latched the door before they had sex, he had been horrified, furious with himself. Saying that anyone could have walked in had been true, but it was more than that. More than he'd been willing to say to her. And thank God he hadn't been able to put it into words, because she was leaving, anyway. It looked like he wasn't going to have to break his vow after all. And that was a good thing. Because he'd just seen firsthand what Theresa had complained about time and time again. When push came to shove—when it really, really counted—the emotions wouldn't come out. They were still bottled up inside of him. Because the specter of his father, of his past, was still holding him hostage in ways that he didn't understand.

Was it just the fear of becoming like him? He wasn't so sure anymore. But he'd held himself in check for so long, that he didn't know what freedom to express himself actually looked like.

It was safer this way, but that didn't mean it was any less painful. In fact, it hurt like hell. It was just that no one but him was able to see it.

So somehow he was going to have to figure out how to work with her—or at least in the same hospital with her—until she was ready to hand in her notice and leave.

That would not be an easy task. But the possibility of her staying here forever would be even more unbearable. Because he was pretty sure—given what had happened so far—they would fall into bed again, if she stayed. It wasn't the cycle he'd originally feared being unable to break. But it might end up being almost as damaging to both of them.

So all he could do was avoid her as much as possible and pray that some cosmic being set the clocks on fast-forward. Once she was gone, things would go back to normal.

At least he hoped that was true.

Kirsten didn't invite Snow to the meeting she had with Gretchen's parents. Instead, she went to it alone, giving Sarah and Bob the results of the MRI and outlining some treatment options that she thought could slow the progression of their daughter's heart failure. But she also honestly told them that Gretchen's best chance for long-term survival, once the meds stopped working, was going to be a heart-lung transplant.

"Will she be able to do PE before the transplant?"

"Before the MRI, I might have said yes, but at this point, we don't want to put any further strain on her heart."

"So it's that bad," her father said. "What kind of timeline are we looking at?"

"I spoke with Dr. Tangredi earlier, and he thinks we've probably got a year and then she'll need a transplant."

Sarah's eyes closed for a second before reopening. "Gretchen is a strong girl. We'll talk to her, but I'm sure she'll want the transplant when the time comes. How do we go about that?"

"Snow… Dr. Tangredi wasn't able to be here today." She didn't tell them it was because she couldn't be in the same room with him right now. Instead, she went on, "I'll contact him and set up an appointment. He can give you a rundown on what happens once a transplant is a necessity. I think you already know, he's an excellent surgeon. One of the best out there. Gretchen will be in excellent hands."

"She's going to want you to be there with her through the process."

Kirsten smiled, even though her heart was breaking. "Of course. I'll be with her for as long as I'm at the hospital."

Unfortunately, that wasn't going to be very long. Not if she could help it.

She'd gotten a hold of her dad and told him the situation, leaving out the part about

Snow and what had happened between them. But her father had always been able to read her like a book, and since they'd done a videoconferencing call, he'd been able to take one look at her face and see that something was wrong. He asked her not to rush into any decisions, that she'd only been at the hospital for a short time.

She'd replied that whether it was Lebanon or another hospital, she couldn't stay at NYC Memorial any longer. He didn't ask why, and Kirsten didn't volunteer any information, but she was pretty sure her dad knew exactly why she needed out of here. It made her feel like such a fool. First Dave and now Snow. Hadn't she once told herself that he couldn't break her heart, because her emotions weren't involved when they'd had sex. What a lie that had been. Because her heart was broken, and there was nothing anyone could do about it at this point.

Her dad told her whenever she returned home, she would be welcomed. He already had a house with three bedrooms, had just hoped he might need the two extras for a son-in-law and grandchildren.

At this point, she didn't see that happening, and she ached for the sadness that would bring her father.

Bob stood, dragging her thoughts back to the present. "We appreciate all you've done for Gretchen. Can you get us an appointment with Dr. Tangredi as soon as possible?"

"Yes, of course I will." She took a couple of prescription forms off her pad and scribbled the medications they would need. "Get these filled and start on them tomorrow. Let me know if there are any problems. One of them is to help regulate the pressure in her lungs and the other one is to help stabilize her heart. I'll let you know as soon as I get that appointment time with Dr. Tangredi."

She shook both of their hands, surprised when Sarah leaned in to hug her instead. Kirsten returned the hug, suddenly needing it with a desperation that surprised her. Then she let go and said her goodbyes. They didn't know this was probably the last time they would see each other, but she did.

As they walked away, she grieved not knowing what Gretchen's final outcome would be. But she'd told the truth. Snow was an excellent surgeon and if anyone could make this miracle happen, it was him.

As far as her own miracle was concerned, there was no surgeon in the world who would be able to fix her shattered heart. Even if there were a transplant that would fix the problem, she was pretty sure the new heart would crumble, too. And the one after that, and the one after that.

Until there were no more hearts left to try.

That was when she decided she wasn't going to wait a week or even a month. She was going to call Snow and ask for an appointment time and then she was going to take a personal leave of absence.

And go home.

Unfortunately, she ran into Nicola just before she reached the inner sanctum of her office.

"Hey, I was just looking for you."

"You were?"

"Yes, do you have time for a coffee? I could use some adult time. I love that baby of mine, but it's just come to the point that I..." Her words faded away as she stared into Kirsten's face. "Hey, what's wrong?"

Then and there, she knew she was going to lose it. She opened her office door and dragged her friend inside. Then she promptly burst into tears.

Nicola put her arm around her shoulder and pulled her over to the chairs that were in front of her desk, then waited until she sat down and thrust a tissue into her hands. "Now, spill. What is it? A patient?"

She shook her head, scrubbing the tissue under her eyes, so angry at herself that she couldn't see straight. How could she let herself get into a situation like this again? Once hadn't been enough to cure her? Evidently not.

Nicola leaned down and looked at her face. "It's Snow, isn't it? I should have known when you came to ask me about him. I'm sorry I didn't realize..."

"I didn't realize, either. Not until—" She shut her eyes. "It doesn't matter. I'm going back to Lebanon."

"What? When?"

"As soon as possible."

With that, she unraveled the whole story for her friend, telling her about Dave and how it seemed like history was repeating itself. How she'd come to care about a man who had no emotions.

"I'm sure that's not true. Snow has emotions. They're just…hidden."

The huge pause before she said that last word struck Kirsten as funny. She giggled. The giggle turning to a laugh that made its way back to tears. "I love him, Nic. But I just can't do—" she waved her hand in a circle and then placed it on her heart "—this. Not again. Please don't try to talk me out of leaving."

"I won't, honey. But please promise me you'll think long and hard about it."

"I already have. And every thought leads back to one of two places. With Snow breaking my heart. Or with me leaving. And I know that the only viable path—the only path where I can come away with any self-respect—is that last one." She reached over and hugged her. "Thank you for everything. I'll never forget how you helped me or gave me your friendship."

"I won't forget you, either, Kirsten. Even though I may not agree with your decision. Let me know if you need anything at all, you hear?"

"Thank you. I will."

CHAPTER TEN

Snow waited for two days before deciding he'd call Kirsten back. Her voice mail had been short and to the point, asking him to please call Sarah and Bob Wilson to make an appointment to talk with them about Gretchen's transplant process. It included their phone number.

He hadn't called them back yet, either. He'd made a huge mistake with Kirsten, but there was no way to fix it now. He'd planned on pulling her aside after the earlier meeting with Gretchen's parents that they were supposed to have together, but she'd never called him to give him a time. Evidently that meeting had already taken place. Without him.

Not that he could blame her. Not after how he'd acted the last time they were together.

He sat there and played with his phone, pulling up her number and then sending it away.

What was wrong with him?

He'd had an emotional response to what Kirsten had said to him that day in his office—after he'd told her about his father. She'd even helped him to see why he'd gone into transplant medicine. That response had driven him to make love to her, putting every ounce of feeling he possessed into it. The sex had been amazing, even with their clothes still on. And he realized then and there that he loved her.

Then he discovered he'd left the door to his office unlocked. But when he fixed it and then turned around to look at Kirsten, his father's voice sounded in his head as clear as day, the words every bit as smug and angry as they'd been that day: "This is what happens when you forget to lock your door, Snowden. Things get broken."

He remembered coming home from Kaleb's house when he was fourteen and finding everything in his room smashed to bits. His mattress had been slashed, clothing ripped apart and his game system had been lying trashed on the ground.

Too late, he realized that the same thing had just happened with Kirsten. The panic room he'd so carefully installed inside of himself was in ruins. Because he'd not only forgotten to lock the door of his office, but he'd also forgotten to lock the door of his heart. And Kirsten came in when he wasn't looking and tore down all of his defenses.

Except casting her in the role of villain had been wrong. So very wrong. Kirsten hadn't destroyed anything. And instead of recognizing that this might be the start of something better and even more beautiful, he'd stood there looking at her like she'd suddenly grown two heads. She hadn't. It had been shock. And the fear that he might mess everything up again, like he'd done with Theresa.

Guess what. He had. And when Kirsten had said she was going to leave, it was like a huge wave of relief poured over him. He wouldn't get the chance to mess things up, because there would be nothing here to destroy. She was leaving. Leaving his office. Leaving his life.

It was a good thing, right?

It wasn't. Because Snow had stood in this office over the last two days and tried to install an even bigger and better lock on his heart. He'd failed. Because all he could think about was Kirsten and how much he wanted her.

"Okay, Snow. Time to call her." Whether she left or not, it didn't change the fact that he loved her. And the only way he would truly be free was to stop bottling everything up inside of him, starting with this. He had to tell her how he felt. And let the chips fall where they may.

He found her number again on his contact list and stared at it for several seconds. Then he pushed the button. It didn't ring. Instead, a weird sound came through, along with a recorded message saying the number was either disconnected or no longer in service.

His mouth went dry, heart suddenly pounding in his chest. He was too late. She'd already left.

Surely not. She said she was going to get her cases all sorted out and it might take a while. But what if it hadn't taken that long.

What if, like Gretchen's case, she'd simply passed them on to someone else.

He hung up, tossing the phone onto his desk. There was no way he was going to be able to find her in Lebanon. He didn't even speak the language and had no idea what city her father lived in.

Staring at the couch where they'd made love, his jaw tightened. So he was just giving up?

It would be the easier way.

Would a transplant surgeon really take that path? He'd always told his patients that the easiest thing to do was let nature take its course. But if they had the grit to take it to the next level, if they would get down in the mud and fight to make it happen, they might just come out on the other side a brand-new person. Transplant surgery was one of the hardest things a patient had to face. It wasn't "the easy way." It was damn hard. But if it worked, it was so very worth it.

Okay. So let's get down in the mud and fight, dammit!

The next step wasn't easy, but if his best friend could admit defeat and give in to love, so could he. Picking his phone back up, he called Kaleb.

"Hey, Snow, what's up?"

"I have kind of a weird question."

His friend went silent, and then he chuckled. "Is it about that pulmonologist that Nicola has been so chummy with?"

"Yes, why?"

"Just wondering why it took you so long to call."

A flare of hope went off in his chest. "Do you know where she is?"

"No, but I know someone who might. Hold on." He heard Kaleb call for his wife.

Nicola came on and didn't give him a chance to speak. "I'm telling you right now, do not mess this up, Snow. Or I'm personally going to come over there and kick your ass."

That made him laugh. "I'll do my best, which is why I called. I take it you know where she's at?"

"She's almost gone. She isn't leaving permanently, if that's what you're asking. But if you don't make it to the airport in an hour, you're going to have to wait for a week before she'll be back." There was a pause. "And that will probably be to pack up her life here.

She didn't tell me why she's leaving so suddenly, but I suspect I'm on the phone with the reason right now, aren't I?"

He swallowed, knowing she didn't expect an answer to that particular question. "What's her flight number?"

"I thought so. And I'm not sure. All I know is she's headed to Lebanon and her flight leaves at seven tonight."

"Thanks, Nicola, I owe you."

"No, you don't. Just do the right thing this time, Snow. For both your sakes."

With that, he ended the call and got up from his desk, shoving his keys and phone into his pocket. And headed out the door.

Kirsten sat in her seat looking out over the terminal. Her flight would start boarding soon. She'd already let her dad know that she was coming home for a visit to do some thinking. As she'd promised, she was not making any hard-and-fast decisions, but whatever the outcome, she would probably not be going back to NYC Memorial. Although she hadn't made the break official yet—simply telling the hospital administrator that she needed a week of personal leave and that she'd handed her cases over to other doctors at the hospital—she couldn't see herself going back. To do so would just be inviting pain back into her life. And that was one thing she was no longer willing to do.

It had been surprisingly easy. Too easy to just up and leave Snow behind.

She amended that. The physical process was easy. But the emotional part had been pure unadulterated hell. Was still hell. She loved the man. But the reality was, he didn't love her. He'd proven that by not even trying to get in contact with her over the last couple of days. She'd canceled her phone service, so that she'd stop staring at it waiting for his call. She was cutting off points of contact, one string at a time. It would be hard, but she'd survive. If she could live through her mom's death, she could live through pretty much anything.

She swallowed. It wasn't the same, though. With her mom, there hadn't been a choice, there'd been no way to hold on to her and keep her here. With Snow it was different. She was making a conscious choice to leave him behind. And each and every day would bring the same choice: to call him or not to call. And with each don't-call decision she made, she had a feeling her heart would break all over again.

If she was in Lebanon, though, that decision would be made easier because the distance would provide an additional barrier.

"Now boarding passengers for Flight 579 to Lebanon. We'll be starting with zone one and working our way back. Those in zone one can come on up."

She still had a ways to go, since she was zone four. After pulling her earbuds from her ears and wrapping them up to put in her bag, she stood, checking to make sure she had everything.

She didn't. But unless she wanted to kidnap Snow and stuff him in the baggage compartment, there was nothing she could do about that.

Glancing at her ticket to find her seat number, she jumped when someone tapped her shoulder. Turning, her heart leaped into her throat when the man she'd just been thinking appeared in the flesh. No. That wasn't right. She blinked to make sure she wasn't imagining it.

God. He was still there. Still staring at her. She started to shake.

"Wh-what are you doing here? How did you even find me?"

He smiled, but it looked strained. "You once asked Nicola if she knew anything about me. Well, I took a page from your book and did the exact same thing. I figured if anyone knew where you were, it would be her."

"Zone two can begin boarding," the loud-speaker called out for the next group to come up.

He glanced at her hand. "What zone are you in?"

It was then that she realized he had a carry-on bag with him. Her emotions tangled up into a ball that lodged in her throat. "What are you doing?"

"We don't have much time. And you have a decision to make." He let go of his bag and took hold of her hands. "I made a terrible mistake, Kirs."

She swallowed. Why was he putting her through this? "I know. We both did, and that's why I decided to—"

"No. My mistake wasn't in what happened

in that office. My mistake was in not admitting then and there that I was in love with you. That I didn't want you to walk out of my office or out of my life."

"But you didn't." Her head was spinning so much that she wasn't quite sure what he was saying. Wait, had he just said…? "Say that again."

"Which part?"

Hope right now was as shaky as her legs had been after that first night she'd spent with him. "You know what part."

"Okay. I love you."

"Zone three is ready for boarding."

"But how? You sure didn't seem like you loved me that day."

"Because I was in shock. I never thought it could happen to me. And then I left my door unlocked and realized it wasn't the only thing I'd forgotten to lock. I'd left my heart wide-open. And you walked right inside."

She could understand that. Understand the fear that came along with it. But what if he suddenly decided he was going to take that padlock and put it on again, locking her on the outside while he hid inside.

"How do I know this won't happen again?"

"Zone four, please come forward for boarding."

The crowd had thinned considerably.

"I can't promise there won't be times when I struggle with things, with showing my emotions, but you have a habit of bringing them out in me even when I'm fighting my hardest against them. No one else has ever been able to do that. Except you. Besides, you'd call me out on it, if I ever tried to pull that kind of crap on you." He glanced to where passports and tickets were being checked. "I'm zone four, as well. So what'll it be?"

"What?"

"I bought a ticket for the same flight, but I'm in a different row. So we can talk here, or I can camp out in the aisle next to your seat and talk to you there."

"Do you even have a passport?"

He pulled it out and brandished it in front of her.

Kirsten couldn't believe this was happening. "What about your job? Did you even ask permission to leave?"

He gave that half smile she loved so much. "There wasn't time. I'm pretty much running on pure emotion right now. And it's actually pretty refreshing."

"That's great, but I have to tell you I'm feeling pretty discombobulated right now."

"Did I ever tell you I love it when you use that word?"

She rolled her eyes. "Give me your ticket."

He frowned. "Why?"

"Trust me?" Her hope had started to stand on its own two feet, its restarted heart now beating on its own.

He handed her the ticket.

She took both of them and walked up to the desk with them, knowing his eyes were watching her the whole way. The attendant at the desk asked if she could help her. "I have two tickets for Lebanon, but I won't be boarding today. Do you need the seat numbers?"

"Yes, thank you."

They made a note of the seats, and Kirsten walked back to where Snow was standing with their luggage. Then, in front of him, she ripped both tickets in half.

He smiled. "I take it we're going to catch a later flight. I do want to go. I want to meet your dad. And the rest of your family." He hesitated, and for the first time, she saw a hint of insecurity in his gaze. "That is, if you feel something for me, too. You haven't said it. That you love me."

She held up the torn tickets. "I think I just did." She wrapped her arms around his neck and kissed him. "Of course I love you. But I can't promise I won't ever want to move back to Lebanon."

"We'll sort that out later. But when we do, we'll make sure we have adjoining seats for the flight. I don't want to be separated from you ever again."

"Me, either." Kirsten looked at the now empty waiting area. "I'll need to call my dad and let him know I won't be on this particular flight."

"Will he be very disappointed?"

"No. He actually told me not to come. To settle whatever it was that was driving this decision first." She laughed, remembering how he'd tried to talk her out of coming home. "And he bought a house with extra rooms that he expects me to fill."

"What?"

"He wants grandchildren, someday, I hate to tell you. I'm pretty sure he knew I was running away from someone, even though I never told him about us." She looped an arm around his waist, letting him lead her over to the window. "You'll like my dad, Snow. He's a good man. A very good man. You remind me so much of him. You're stoic. A hard worker. But most of all you're a protector of those who need it the most."

Snow didn't say anything, but when she glanced up at him and saw a muscle working furiously in his jaw and his glassy eyes, she knew why. And this was one time she wasn't going to complain. Because Snow was learning to deal with his emotions, and she was going to let him take baby steps. All the baby steps he needed. Because that's what love did.

Arm in arm, they stood there as the doors closed on Flight 579 bound for Lebanon. The plane was pushed backward so it could turn to taxi onto the runway. They were still standing there when it took off, flying farther and farther into the distance until they could no longer see it.

Snow kissed the top of her head, and she smiled up at him, her heart so full she could barely contain her joy.

They'd almost lost each other. Might have been separated forever.

Except Kirsten now believed in miracles. Because she was standing next to the man who regularly made them happen.

EPILOGUE

"WE WOULD LIKE to introduce Dr. Snowden Tangredi and Dr. Kirsten Nadif-Tangredi. Please give them a warm welcome."

As everyone clapped, Kirsten walked up to the lectern. Snow loved everything about his wife's country. The food was crazy good. The people were ridiculously friendly. And his father-in-law was an amazing man, just like Kirs had said he was. Snow wasn't like him at all. Not yet. But he aspired to be like him, one day.

As his wife stood at the podium giving her portion of the lecture on innovative treatment plans for cystic fibrosis, he admired the curve of her back and her glossy black hair, which was pulled up into a tight bun. And when she turned slightly to the side to acknowledge the session's moderator, he caught sight of a slight curve in her abdomen that most would not take notice of. But he did. They'd discovered a month ago that Kirsten was pregnant. They were on their way to putting the first crib in his father-in-law's extra rooms. And he couldn't be happier.

Snow hadn't been sure about coming to the conference because of the pregnancy, but Kirs insisted she would be fine.

This was their second time participating in the International Medical Professionals Forum that was hosted here in Lebanon. And both times, Kirs had stood beside him as he spoke, translating his words into Arabic, so the audience could understand him. He loved hearing her converse in her native language and was working on learning it himself. And he loved meeting other specialists in his field. They had a lot to learn from each other.

Both he and Kirs had talked about joining Doctors Without Borders and helping in whatever ways they could. Her father had already said he would be happy to watch his grandchild whenever they needed him to.

And when they got back to the States, they

promised Gretchen's parents that they would come to her birthday party. She'd gotten her heart-lung transplant last year and was now participating in PE, using her newfound knowledge in kinesiology to help her fellow students get the most out of their training. Her dream was to someday be a coach. Or a transplant surgeon. That had made him smile.

Snow looked out over the audience. Kirsten's dad was out there somewhere, although with the lights, he couldn't see him. It was obvious, though, that he was very proud of his daughter. Not only of her accomplishments in the medical field, but also of her as a person. A compassionate, loving, emotion-filled person.

It had been an adjustment getting used to everything—getting used to expressing himself. But he was learning.

The locks on his doors were history. Oh, not completely. They had what Kirs considered to be a reasonable number of safeguards. Even the extra lock on his office door had been taken off—the hole left where the mechanism had once been was covered with a red wooden heart, as a nod to his specialty. And to Kirsten.

And, hell, if he wasn't the happiest man in this room. Or at least tied for first place.

He had everything he'd never known he wanted but now realized he couldn't live without: a wife who loved him, despite all his faults, a baby who would be loved *by* him and a large extended family that was just as exuberant as his beautiful bride. And his mom, who'd welcomed Kirsten with open arms. Her healing had come years ago, and she'd thanked her new daughter-in-law— when she thought he wasn't listening, of course—for helping Snow find the healing that he so desperately needed.

Kirs glanced at him with a smile and spoke to the audience before translating it into English for him. "And now I'd like to introduce my husband, the love of my life and regular worker of miracles, transplant surgeon Snowden Tangredi."

He smiled as he made his way to the podium, stopping to give his wife's hand a quick squeeze as he passed her. His heart filled with love and gratitude. She may have introduced him as a "worker of miracles," but that wasn't true. Because the real worker of miracles was carrying his child. How did he know she could perform miracles? Because with a single kiss, Kirs had taken Snow's tragic, damaged heart and somehow made it brand-new.

* * * * *